S

Death at the Corral

Wild bull-rider Buck Bradley aimed to win the Oklahoma rodeo championships and was catching up fast on his rival, Dusty Roberts. Buck also had eyes for the rancher's beautiful daughter, Jane Merriman, who was looking for top prizes on her superb Appaloosa.

But who was behind the slaughter of ranch-hands and the poisoning and theft of their horses? Rich oilman Robert Rudge was the main suspect. He had big money riding on Dusty and had vowed that his daughter Rachel would win the women's cup. But how could Buck prove this? This and many other questions had to be answered before it all climaxed in an explosion of treachery and violence.

101 ALFN	3/07
102 RIPY	
103 BELP	
104 HEAN	
105 DUFD	
106 SOMC	
107 MCV 1	5/03
108 MCV 2	4/04
109 MCV 3	2/05
110 BEL M1	
111 BEL M2	
112 ALF M	

Death at the Corral

JOHN DYSON

A Black Horse Western

ROBERT HALE · LONDON

Typeset by Derek Doyle & Associates, Liverpool.
Printed and bound in Great Britain by
Antony Rowe Limited, Wiltshire.

One

Buck Bradley swung up over the wooden rails of the chute where Angelface was stomping and snorting and stood poised to one side so the bull couldn't crush his legs in their batwing chaps. The noise from the excited crowd packed around the arena at Tulsa annual rodeo suddenly calmed into an expectant hush. To date, no man had stayed on the big brindled bull for the full term of eight seconds, but if any man could do it it was the lean and rangy cowboy who was now preparing to get on his back.

'Careful does it, mister,' his part-Comanche handler, Reno, whispered, as he hooked up the free end of the bull rope from under the beast's belly, pulled it taut and handed it to Bradley. 'He's a twister.'

'Aw, I was born in a twister an' I been creatin' hell ever since,' Buck bragged with a tense grin. 'There ain't no bull that cain't be rode.'

He took the rope end and carefully began to wrap it around the back of his right hand and over the palm, weaving it through the third and fourth fingers of his worn leather gloves, pounding it in firm. He glanced across the arena to the dark-haired girl, his boss's daughter, who was standing leaning on the rails near the judges' box. She was still in her spangled finery, the flowing dress she had worn to ride side saddle on her feisty Appaloosa stallion to win the equitation event. His grin widened as he met her eyes. 'Nor no woman neither,' he growled.

The big-gutted judge got to his feet and his voice boomed out through the megaphone in his hand. 'Well, folks, we got Angelface, the biggest, baddest, cross-Brahma we ever done seen weighing in at two thousand and twenty pounds. Buck Bradley is twenty-five years old, five feet ten without his high-heeled boots, and weighs one hundred and fifty pounds. He's a cowboy from south of Oklahoma Territory and he aims to be Horseman of the Year. Y'all know he's done miracles so far in the bronc-bustin' line at other festivals, but can he stay on the back of this bull for more than eight seconds? Can any man? In just a moment, folks, we're gonna find out.'

Jane Merriman had laid aside her hard, gold-painted helmet with its trailing streamers and donned a sassy straw sombrero against the glare of the setting sun, the great red glowing ball that was sinking low into the prairie, and watched the man tensed for action. When he had looked deliberately across at her his eyes had seemed to clash sparks off her own and she had to admit her heart had lurched. But she did not care for his follow-up raunchy grin, so high and mighty, as if he had her in his sights like some little dogie he was planning to cut out of a herd. Well, let him try.

Her father had taken on Buck Bradley that

summer as one of the drovers on their ranch on the understanding that he would be given time off to compete in the various rodeos that were all the rage around the territory. She had the idea her crippled father, a former rodeo rider himself, wanted Buck to go along as minder to his daughter. But it had become obvious that Buck had more than minding on his mind. Oh, yes, she had met his kind before.

Bradley had built up quite a reputation as a bull-rider and horse-racer in the territorial journals, and probably, she suspected, among the simple country girls who flocked in with their families to see the show. She had noted the way he swaggered into the arena, swinging those tattered chaps, and how his infectious grin lit up adoring, saucy smiles on the girls' faces. 'They're welcome to take their chances with him,' Jane had told her coloured maid, Sally, 'but he needn't get the idea he is going to rope this filly.'

And, yet, she tensed inside with concern as she watched Bradley jerk his Stetson tight down over his brow, his fawn hair, badly in need of a cut, curled over the back knot of the fancy bandanna around his throat, his face serious now. Could he, she wondered, ride the massive bull?

Buck had studied the bull at several rodeos and knew every evil move he made. The previous year he had had the bad luck to draw him at the finals in Oklahoma City, and the fiery old gladiator had tossed him almost as soon as he was out of the chute. Angelface had caught him like a falling pancake, tossed him some more and badly gored his side. It had put him not only out of the contest but out of work most of the winter. Once again he had drawn the short straw. It looked like they were fated to fight. But he was determined this time to conquer him.

He gritted his teeth as he lowered himself onto the Brahma's hurricane deck, with Reno steadying his shoulder. He suddenly felt the heat and power of the bull between his thighs and his heart began pumping with excitement. All he could do now was to hang on and to hope for some of God's sweet luck. 'Let him go,' he gritted out.

The chute door swung open and it was as if the air was sucked out of his lungs as Angelface kicked for the sky, descending stiff-legged to jar every bone in the rider's body. Buck was tossed back and forth like a rag doll on his back. And then Angelface was going into his twisting, bucking spin, and a paroxysm of belly rolls.

One . . . two . . . three . . . four . . . Jane Merriman mentally counted, as if they were the slowest seconds that ever passed. Yes, six . . . seven . . . he was hanging on, he was going to make it.

'Ah!' There was a loud sigh from the crowd as Bradley hit the dust. Had he made it? No, he was a half-second away from the final count. And he was in trouble as the bull turned and tried to stomp him into the dirt. Buck Bradley rolled away as the clowns ran in, flapping capes to distract the angry, eye-blazing critter who was swinging his vicious horns. They dodged and darted, tried to get him roped as Bradley vaulted over the high corral rail.

By sheer chance, rather than design, he landed beside Jane Merriman, almost knocking her to one side. He caught her arm to steady her, and himself, and grinned his lecherous grin. 'Hi! How did I do?'

There was applause, but not enough, and he knew the bull had beaten him again before she shook her head, her blue eyes regarding him seriously from beneath the brim of her hat. 'You nearly made it, cowboy, but not quite.'

'There's always another day,' he smiled. 'Angelface, he was born to buck. Me I was born to—'

'Yes,' she interrupted, before he could complete the rhyming couplet, if that was what he intended, and she wouldn't put it past him. 'I'm sure you were. But not with me.'

She could feel his large left hand gripping her arm, firm but also gentle, as if testing a fruit he planned to pluck, his eyes challenging hers. She tossed her shoulder, shaking him off. 'You'll have to do better than that, won't you?' And, with a swirl of her long, ruched dress, she turned and made her way out through the throng.

Buck Bradley watched her go, the sway of her hips in the tight dress. 'Whoo-ee!' He stroked his jaw and gave a long, appreciative whistle. 'Ya know, I think she really likes me.'

Buck eased the glove from his right hand with a wince of pain. He had fallen badly and although he was still flying high with the excitement of the ride, his blood pounding through him, he was a shade worried that he might have injured his wrist. No – he exercised his long fingers and thumb back and forth – nothing broken, just a sprain. He gave another whistle through his teeth, of relief this time. He depended on his right-hand grip.

Without it he would be out of the championships, maybe for ever.

'Here's your hat,' Reno called, tossing it to him. It had been caved in by one of the bull's big cloven hooves. 'Lucky your head weren't in it.'

'Yeah.' Buck punched it into shape, rolled the brim up along the sides the way he liked it. 'Try to ruin my best felt Stetson, would he? I'm gonna tame that brute one of these days.'

'I believe you. Nobody else would. Lets hope he don't tame you.'

'Pah! No way.' Buck made a downturned grimace of contempt, maybe to hide the fear every rodeo rider harboured. There were cowboys he knew who had been killed, crippled, and one, kicked in the head, who had been turned into a silent, shuffling zombie. A man had to conquer that fear, keep flying high, otherwise it was all over. 'You're a cheerful bastard, aincha? It's time for the prize-giving. That's what we're here for. You ready?'

'Sure, just gotta git the bulls penned up.'

Buck had done well in the three-day Tulsa rodeo, he and his partner, Reno, beating Dusty Roberts's score in the bull-roping and bull-dogging events to take first prize. He was neck-and-neck now in the bull-riding, but Buck had eaten Dusty's dust in the horse races, coming third in the main half-mile race, which he put down to being boxed in by a couple of Dusty's pals. 'That ain't gonna happen again,' he swore.

As the sun set and tar flares were lit around the arena, all the contestants gathered for a grand parade led by Tulsa town band, banging their drums and oompah-pahing away. Then the winners' names were called out and they rode forward to receive their cash prize, rosette or silver cup from leading citizen Robert Rudge, or his wife, Rowena, a handsome, well-built lady in a flouncy dress and magnificent hat.

Buck watched with admiration as Jane Merriman, graceful in her long dress, golden helmet and streamers cantered the Appaloosa forward to take the ladies' challenge cup. She had pipped the Rudges' daughter, Rachel, by six points. 'Look at Rachel giving her the evil eye,' Buck drawled. 'She don't like havin' her nose put outa joint. Nor does her daddy.'

There was nothing graceful about Bradley's approach to the stadium. Always the showman, he raced around the arena on his quarter horse, Red Desert, then charged like a bullet towards the judges' podium, giving a wild, screeching, rebel yell. A few feet from the folks in the decorated box he leaned back in the saddle and spun the horse around on the spot, kicking up a plume of dust. Buck grinned at Rowena Rudge and she responded with a wide smile, tossing him a rose from the bouquet on her lap. He took off his hat with an affected sweeping motion, tucked the rose in the hatband, and raised it in salute to the roar of applause as he raised Red on his backlegs, his fore-hooves flailing in a dance of triumph. He had trained him well. And he knew how to play a crowd, how to get maximum headlines.

'Well, folks,' Rudge bellowed through the loudhailer, 'here's one cowboy who's cock-a-hoop, but he's still riding behind our local boy, Dusty Roberts, and I cain't see that altering in the Oklahoma champeen-ships.'

Buck snatched the loud-hailer from Rudge's hand and roared out, 'Dusty better watch out. There's a cold blizzard coming in and I'm riding up ahead of it. Be warned, I'm gonna freeze him out. Where I come from, on the borders with Texas, we *know* how to ride.'

He tossed the loudhailer back to Rudge and leaned over to accept his rosettes from Rowena. Rudge scowled. He didn't like the wink Bradley gave his wife.

'You've got yourself an admirer,' Jane said, icily, as he cantered across and drew up beside her.

'Yep.' He took off his hat, shook his hair out of his eyes, adjusted the rose in the band. 'It's purty obvious you don't wanna be my number one, Miss Merriman, you bein' the boss's daughter an' all that. So, I guess I gotta look elsewhere.'

'It doesn't worry you that she's married?'

'Nope.' He met her blue eyes, a tad guiltily. He didn't want to hurt her, but he was not a man accustomed to being celibate for long. 'She may be a bit long in the tooth and broad at the beam, but I like the looks of her and I guess she likes the look of me.'

'You ought to be more careful. Rudge looks to me like a jealous man.'

'Don't you worry none, Jane,' Buck muttered, as he watched Dusty go up and take the big gold race challenge cup from Rowena's hands. 'I ain't likely to be gittin' to know her tonight. And tomorrow we're headin' back to your daddy's ranch. Hey, come on, Jane, what say we all splash out at the Grand Junction hotel, celebrate our triumphs? We done well this time. Your daddy'll be proud of you.'

'No thanks,' she said, as she turned Snow Storm away. 'But I'm sure Mrs Rudge would be glad to raise a glass with you.'

'You goin' for a gargle?' Buck called to Reno as they stabled their horses.

'Sure am, soon as I get this bridle repaired. Where ya gonna be?'

'Along at The Robbers' Roost, where else?' It was the hottest low-spot in town, drinking, dancing, music, gaming into the early hours, with a host of little prairie nymphs who wouldn't say no to any rodeo rider, not least one of the most famed on the Oklahoma circuit. Not like that stuck-up fancypants, Jane Merriman.

Buck ran fingers through his thick and dusty hair, rammed his hat down over his brow and debated whether to strap on his gunbelt with its long barrelled Smith & Wesson .44 revolver. Tulsa by-laws ordained that it would have to be handed in at the door of any saloon. Why bother? He didn't have any enemies. Or so he thought. 'Nah.' He tucked it away beneath the straw in a corner beside his soogans and saddle where he would later stretch out beside Red Desert. He hitched his thumbs each side of the big brass buckle on the belt of his levi jeans and, his chaps swinging, headed out into the throng.

'Hi, there, Buck,' a youth called. 'You ain't never gonna catch Dusty Roberts.'

'I wouldn't bet money on that, mister.' Bradley grinned, used to such banter. But he knew that whatever happened over the next month or so at a couple

13

of local rodeos where they were due to appear, it was going to be a close run thing at the finals.

It had been a long hot summer travelling to rodeos and shows, large and small, in the far-flung reaches of Oklahoma Territory – Vinita, Freedom, Enid, Poteau, Ronca, Broken Bow and Elk City, to mention a few. Jane, he and Reno had all made a name and some cash for themselves. It would be good to get back to the Merriman ranch and rest up for a while.

The bustling town of Tulsa was one of the first in the new Oklahoma Territory to organize a big fair on a regular basis. There was a show ring for local farmers to show off their fine fatstock and where cowboys from the outlying ranches could display their skills at bronco-riding and bull-dogging. Gradually it had become more professional with contestants from all parts chasing the prize money. A half-mile circular track had been built for spring and fall pony races, buggy and harness events, and one of the most popular classes introduced was for females to show off their jumping and horse control.

Since before the Civil War this vast area had been designated as Indian Territory and had become a dumping ground for tribes from all over the continent. Delawares from the far north-east coast, Modocs from California in the west, were each allotted pieces of ground, mingling, not always too well, with Comanches from the plains, Kickapoos from the north, Seminoles from Florida and so forth. There were also the so-called civilized tribes like the Cherokee and Choctaw, who had lived on this land a good deal longer. They were natural horse people and they, too, loved to show off their prowess at their own religious pow-wows.

However, since the war, this Indian land of plains, forests and rivers had become not only a magnet for fugitives and outlaws, but the envy of surrounding whites. Gradually the Indians' rights had been whittled away, and the Nations opened to general settlement, culminating, memorably, in the run for the Cherokee Strip when thousands on horseback, in buggie, or on foot, raced to stake their claims. New townships grew up overnight. Now in the 1890s, the territory was a thriving mix of many nationalities.

Tulsa City – until recently sleepy Tulsey Town – was one of the fastest growing communities, particularly since oil had been discovered on Osage lands and developed by white men. One of the biggest oil barons was Robert Rudge, who had acquired his holdings by devious means and deals with the Osage, and now had a host of nodding donkeys pumping up oil much in demand in the industrial East. He had seen where the future lay and had built his own railroad to export the crude oil to civilization.

With his newfound wealth Rudge had aspirations to be the leading light of Oklahoma society, not only for himself and his business connections, but for his glamorous green-eyed wife, Rowena, and their daughter, seventeen-year-old Rachel, a keen horse rider. He had given her the finest horses money could buy in the territory, intending that she should take the honour of being Horsewoman of the Year at the Oklahoma City rodeo in the late fall. But he had been surprised and alarmed to note that day's performance at the Tulsa Rodeo by the girl called Jane Merriman on her magnificent Appaloosa stallion, Snow Storm.

'By hook or by crook, Rachel's going to win the Oklahoma finals,' Rudge mused to his wife, that evening as he dressed for dinner. 'I'm going to send for Snake and his boys.'

'Do you think that's wise?' Rowena asked. 'Isn't that asking for trouble?'

'I've promised Rachel that cup and she's going to get it.' Rudge glowered at his wife as he fixed his gold studs. 'And I've got a hell of a lot of cash riding on Dusty Roberts. He's got to win, too. Something's got to be done. I didn't like the look of that cowboy Buck Bradley. He didn't ride Angelface the distance, but he got damn close.'

'Mmm?' The bosomy Rownea Rudge, with her pile of chestnut curls, licked her lips as she applied rouge, and admired her semi-clad image in the dressing mirror. She smiled to herself and murmured, 'I rather liked the look of him, myself.'

'What was that?' Rudge grunted, as he tied his cravat.

'Nothing, dear. You do what you think best.'

'Yeah, well, it's time that no-good cowboy had another accident.'

TWO

Snake Stevens, in his glistening black leather jacket and pants, his silver-toed boots, and low-crowned black hat with a rattler-skin band, looked much like the reptile after whom he had been named; long, sinuous and deadly. He rode into town on his black thoroughbred, pushing carelessly through the crowds, accompanied by his two sidekicks, Ace Weston, a young, card-sharping cowboy, and Danny McCafferty, a beefy, red-faced jack-of-all-trades, most of them illegal.

They climbed from their horses outside the Robbers' Roost, hitched them to the rail and swaggared up the steps to the batwing doors. As was his custom, the cadaverous-faced Snake paused before he stepped inside, his eyes in their narrowed lids observing the noisy throng for any sign of a U.S. marshal, or an enemy with an old score to settle. Men were pressed shoulder-to-shoulder six-deep along the mahogany bar. Around the gaming tables, roulette, blackjack and faro, was a collection of farmers, cowboys, ranchers and shopkeepers, with, here and there, fancily attired professional gamblers, in frock-coats and cross-over vests, who followed the rodeos and fleeced the punters of their dollars. That is, what loose cash the resident hookers didn't get their sticky fingers on.

Snake's long fingers hung loosely over the butt of the silver-engraved Remington revolver in the holster of his bullet-studded belt. He, too, had the air of a professional – a professional killer. Perceiving no threat to his safety, he nodded to his companions to hand in their guns and shoulder a path for him through to the bar.

'Hey, who you pushin'?' a farmer protested, but when he turned and saw Stevens and his bodyguards he stepped quickly aside.

The bar-keep, Hal Robinson, gave him precedence over all the thirsty men demanding to be served, reached for a bottle of whiskey and slid it across with three tumblers. 'Rudge wants to see you.'

Snake carefully removed his black gloves, tipped back his hat to hang on his back, and ran fingers through his greasy black hair. 'Where is he?'

'Over at the Grand Junction Hotel having dinner with Rowena and Rachel.'

'I'll find him later.'

'He said it was urgent, to tell you so if I saw you.'

'I'm in no hurry. Rudge might own you and this joint, Hal, but he don't own me.' With that Stevens jerked out the cork from the bottle with his teeth, spat it away, and filled the tumblers with liquor. He picked up his own glass, took a slug, winced, and turned, leaning the small of his back against the bar to survey the throng. 'Get an eyeful of them whores,' he leered, his teeth glinting beneath his thin lips and neat pencil moustache. 'Who do they think they are?'

Up on the podium a professor of ivories was rattling out a fast, furious tune, amplified by a Mexican blasting away on a battered trumpet, and two of his fellow countrymen, strumming like fury at their guitars as a chorus of dancing girls cart-wheeled and high-kicked, showing off their frilly drawers, swishing their scarlet satin petticoats, their squeals and screams adding to the cacophony.

'They calls it the Can Can,' McCafferty announced knowledgeably. 'It's all de rage in Paris, France. Dat's across de ocean, yuh know.'

'I know where Paris, France, is.' Snake took another slug of the whiskey. 'They ain't likely to be doin' it in Paris, Texas, are they?'

'It's been banned by de pope, it has,' McCafferty mused, 'but it don't seem to be stoppin' dese girls. Just look at dat, now!'

'Yeah, and how about those hicks in front of the pode?' Snake nodded towards a knot of old men and gormless ranch boys gathered at the edge of the stage gazing up at the knicker-flashing harlots as if in seventh heaven. 'You'd think they'd never seen under a gal's skirts before.'

'Look who's come in,' Ace sneered, as Reno, a half-Comanche, a beaded headband holding back his thick, shoulder-length black hair from his savage countenance, pushed through the crowd towards them. 'Do they serve his sort in here?'

'They serve anybody who's got a dollar,' Snake drawled. 'This is Indian Territ'ry, ain't it?'

'Yeah, well, I agree with Gen'ral Sheridan,' Ace spat out. 'The only good Injin's a dead un.'

'Howdy, Reno!' a cowboy standing beside them

19

yelled. 'Get your peepers on them gals. I bet your Comanche pals never hollered so loud. What you havin', boy? Better have a beer. You know the whiskey sends you crazy.'

Snake Stevens turned to eye the cowboy. 'Hey, ain' you that rodeo rider, Bradley?'

'Thass me. An' I ain't ashamed to admit it. Nor too proud to allow you to buy me and my handler, Reno, two more beers.'

Snake nodded at the 'keep. 'Fill 'em up. Best of luck, Bradley, but you ain't got a hope in hell of catching up with Dusty Roberts. He's ten points ahead of you. He rides like he's glued to the saddle. That boy has the fortune of the devil.'

Buck blew the froth off the top of his pint glass of beer and grinned as it flecked Stevens' fancy silk shirt. He pointed a finger at the gunman's face. 'Hey, are those caterpillars climbing up your cheeks?'

Snake stroked one of his sideburns, his right hand closing in to a fist. 'Just watch your mouth, smartass.'

'Yeah,' Ace put in. 'We don't like comedians.'

Buck grinned again with drunken bravado. 'You gents, you really frighten me.' He raised his glass to them and took a long swig of the beer, thumping it back onto the counter, staring at it, before saying, 'They oughta call him Lucky Roberts. But he's heading for a fall one of these days. No man can stay that lucky forever. If that sounds like sour grapes you better watch me in our next quarter-mile race.'

'Yeah?' Snake gave a contemptuous laugh. 'All you're gonna smell is his pony's gas.' With that, he turned his back on Bradley. 'Beer! Huh! Thass all that loser will ever be able to afford.'

20

Reno gripped Buck's arm as he saw him tense. 'Leave it, mister. Doncha know who that is?'

'No, who is he?'

'Snake Stevens, one of the deadliest shots in the territory,' Reno muttered. 'I seen him in action.'

Buck shrugged and held onto the bar to steady himself. 'Big deal.'

'That was great!' Jane called to her friend and helper, Sally Sago, as she cantered her stallion, Snow Storm, into the livery. She had taken the opportunity of the sunset's afterglow to ride her Appaloosa across the prairie for a mile or so. It had been good to wind down after the concentration of the contest, to give the stallion his head, to let him go. As soon as she was out of sight of the town where modesty decreed that a young lady should ride side-saddle, she had hoicked up her skirts and straddled the horse, riding the way she liked to ride back at the ranch. It was good to feel his surge of power between her legs as she balanced her toes in the stirrups, leaning forward over his neck and his flying mane, the prairie wind streaming through her own hair. 'A good gallop is the most stimulating, exciting experience in God's creation,' she said, as she jumped down and led the sweat-flecked Snow Storm into a stall.

'Sho, maybe,' her curly-haired black maid, Sally, replied with a big flashing grin. 'Yo' would say that, but that's 'cause you ain' nevuh had a man like Buck Bradley 'tween yo' legs.'

'Lord, Sally, do you have to be so crude?' Jane uncinched the stallion and threw his saddle across the stall rail. 'I can assure you the day a man does

21

that to me again will be my wedding day. And it won't be Buck Bradley.'

'Why?' Sally asked. 'What yo' got aginst him? Cain't yo' see he's crazy for ya?'

Jane considered this information as she filled a water bucket to rub the horse down and Sally tossed him some fresh hay. 'Oh, he's OK. He's a nice enough guy. But, you know yourself, he's just a drifter. He's not marriage material.'

'Jest 'cause you got burned once, it don't mean every man's gonna be a heel. You gotta give 'em a chance, gal.'

Jane's face took a saddened, serious air as she combed the tangles out of the stallion's mane, and she remembered Chris, the tall, easygoing cowboy who had arrived to work at her father's ranch two years before. Yes, she had fallen for him in a big way. She had believed him when he said he felt the same way about her. All that kissing under the stars in the moonlight until she had succumbed to his pleas and he had seduced her in the hayloft. Yes, it had been thrilling and wonderful, until one morning she had gone out into the yard to find that Chris had saddled up and ridden on his way. It took some while for her to accept that he was gone and was not coming back. The only good thing was he had not left her a little baby to remember him by.

'No, I've had my fill of wandering cowboys. If I ever get married it will be to a solid, decent, honest man, who shares my love of horses. Not some rodeo rider. To tell the truth, Sally, it horrifies me to see those poor, ill-treated, demented broncos, made to kick and buck the way they do. How could I bear to be with a man who inflicts that kind of cruelty?'

'Your daddy used to be a rodeo rider.'

'Yes, I guess he did. And look at him. They brought him home one day on a stretcher.'

'Miz Jane, brighten up. Hey, how 'bout you an' me go see the town?'

'No, I'd rather stay in, Sally.'

'Hey, the contest's over. It's time to celebrate, Janey. Let's have some fun, listen to the music, see the bright lights. Tomorrow we'll all be heading back to the backwoods.'

So, much against her will, Jane had allowed herself to be persuaded and, after supper at their boarding-house, they had freshened up and stepped out to see the town. It was certainly lively. On a corner a group of Indians in feathered finery were having a pow-wow. Some Czechs who worked in the oilfields were in national dress holding a folk dance. A half-naked, fire-eating busker was performing his tricks. And settlers of numerous nationalities were thronging the streets.

'Hey,' Sally called, peeping over the batwing doors of The Robbers' Roost. 'Won't you jest listen to that piano? Look at dem gals doin' dat dance. It's scan-d'lous. Les go in.'

'No.' Jane shied like a horse refusing a jump. 'It's not respectable—'

'Aw, c'mon.' Sally, in her tight-busted dress of blue gingham grabbed Jane's arm. 'There's loads of 'spectable farm gals and folks in dere. It's rodeo. They all gotta let their hair down once a year. Nobody don't care.'

At which, she led the way into the crowded, noisy saloon, prodding men's buttocks with her parasol requesting them to make way, while Jane followed more demurely. The rowdy Westerners grinned and exaggeratedly beckoned them through.

'Hey, howdy, gals,' Buck Bradley yelled, as they reached the bar. 'You're slummin', aincha? I ain't so sure Mr Merriman would approve of you bein' in this house of what you might call ill-repute.'

'He don't mourn what he don't see, do he?' Sally slipped an arm around Reno's waist. It was obvious to Jane she had planned this chance encounter. 'We gonna jig, ain' we, honey?'

'What you having to drink?' Buck asked.

'I'll have one of those new Coca Colas,' Jane shouted above the din. 'If I may?'

'Sure, have a shot of rum in it.' He smiled, warmly, at her. 'Might make you lose your inhibitions.'

'No, thanks. I'm not planning on that.' She watched Sally and the stern-faced Reno bobbing about amid a throng of sweat-streamed dancers. 'Do they call that dancing?' But, despite herself, she couldn't stop her foot tapping to the jingling, blaring music, if music it could be called. 'It looks more like a wrestling match.'

Buck studied the girl in her straw sombrero, the piercing blue of her eyes, the high cut of her cheek-bones, the shimmering black hair tumbling about her slim neck and shoulders, the determined jut of her chin and her lissom figure in the long show dress. He passed her drink. 'Look at them two glued together. You couldn't git a cigareet paper 'tween their bellies. At least li'l Sal knows how to have fun.'

'Meaning I don't?'

'You wanna git in there, too?' he asked, grabbing

24

her around the waist and pulling her into him. 'Let's go.'

'Look! No! Mind my drink!' she protested, trying to break away from him. 'Let me go!'

'Aw, c'mon, Jane. Let's party.'

'For God's sake! I'm too hot already. Quit it!' she cried, trying to break free from his arms without spilling her drink. 'I don't like being man-handled.'

'Jane, why you acting so hoity-toity? You know you want to.'

'Not with you I don't.'

'Hey, squit-face, you heard the li'l gal.' A huge, hairy mountain man suddenly loomed up beside them. Eyes like black buttons in bloodshot whites peered out of a tangle of hair. A whiskey-enflamed nose and pouting pink lips protruded from a greasy beehive of beard. His massive shoulders and chest were clothed in a torn, filthy and faded pink under-vest and his huge hams were encased by cowhide pants which hung in tatters at his calves over the tops of his boots. 'She don't want *you*.'

The giant clawed his great palm at Bradley's face and pushed him sprawling away and with his other arm he hauled Jane into him. 'You come with me, li'l gal. You gonna be my squaw.'

The stench of the man, stale sweat, hairy filth and woodsmoke, was almost overpowering as Jane's face was pressed inot his chest.

'Get off me!' she screamed. 'Leave me alone!'

Buck got to his feet, edged towards them, and aimed a swinging blow of his fist at the mountain man's jaw. 'Aagh!' he cried as he connected and it juddered like electricity through his sprained wrist. A retch of pain on his face, he stood and shook his limp hand. The giant had hardly flinched. He pulled a huge Bowie knife from his belt and waved it belligerently, clamping a brawny forearm over Jane's throat.

As the saloon fell silent and folks craned to see what the screaming was about, Reno took a flying leap and landed on the giant's back, trying to put a headlock on him. The mountain man roared and tossed him off, slashing blood from Reno's arm as he fell. Buck picked up a chair and smashed it across the man's fat shoulders, but he hardly seemed to notice. However, he pointed the knife at Bradley and growled, 'I ever meet you agin, half-pint, I'm gonna cut your tripes out an' eat your liver the way my grandaddy used to do. Liver-eatin' Johnson was his name. He had six squaws and killed three hundred Crows who tried to git him. He ate all their livers, he did. Thas why we Johnsons're so strong.'

'Put that gal down, Johnson,' Buck rapped out, 'and don't be such a damned fool. You could hang for this.' But he was unarmed and he didn't feel as confident as his words sounded as he met Jane's pleading blue eyes.

'Do something,' she gasped out. 'You can't just let him take me.'

The six-foot-six giant had begun backing away with her towards the doors. 'You're comin' with me, missy. You gonna be my squaw. Nobody ain't gonna stop me.'

Snake Stevens leaned on the bar coolly watching the activity, a smile hovering on his thin lips. Ace was pulling out a revolver, secreted in his topcoat, as if about to take a pot-shot at Johnson, but Snake stayed his hand. Everybody else in the saloon seemed to be frozen in motion. Buck looked around helplessly, at a loss as to what to do. They watched the hairy mountain man back out of the swing doors, his knife at the girl's throat. Buck was the first out on the sidewalk and saw the giant hurrying away, buttocks wobbling down the crowded main street, dragging Jane with him. He jumped into the saddle of somebody's waiting horse, unhitched it, snatched a lariat from the saddle horn, and began whirling it as he sent the pony sprinting forward after them, scattering people like skittles. He dropped the noose over Johnson's head, jerking the rope end tight around the saddle horn and sped on past. When the rope tightened with a twang, Buck sat deep in the saddle and took the strain, looking back, seeing Johnson toppled, but still hanging onto the struggling Jane as he was dragged along through the dust. Buck let the cow pony take the pull, leaped down and stomped the heel of his boot into the giant's thick throat. He jerked the rope tighter and heard him gurgle, his little pink tongue sticking out as he struggled. Buck stomped his boot on his wrist and he released the knife. The rodeo rider snatched it up and stuck it into the man's bearded throat. 'Let her go or I'll kill you,' he shouted into the man's face.

After what seemed like an eternity, the twenty-stone man finally released his hold on Jane and Buck pulled her up. He held her to him as she shivered in his arms and they watched other men pile into Johnson, kicking and beating him, overpowering him by sheer numbers and dragging him towards a sturdy oak tree. A man threw the end of the rope over a bough and it was likely they would have lynched him hadn't the town sheriff arrived to take over and escort Johnson at the point of a shotgun back to the hoosegow.

'You're OK now. It's all over,' Buck consoled her. 'They're locking him up.'

'I thought . . . I thought nobody would stop him, that they would let him take me,' she whispered, hoarsely. 'I thought he . . . .'

'Yeah, well he didn't, did he? An' he ain't gonna. All that big bastard'll do is rot in jail for a month or two.'

'Buck, I'm scared. He'll get out. He'll come and get me.'

'No; didn't you smell his whiskey stink? He was mad drunk. Most like when he wakes up in the mornin' he won't remember a durn thing. Come on, I'll take you back to where you're staying.'

Sally and Reno, nursing his bleeding forearm, wandered back with them to the lodging-house. 'That brute,' Sally chattered on. 'I slashed at him with my brolly but he kicked me away. He was waving that knife like a madman. There was nuthin' we could do. It was Buck saved you, Janey.'

'Yes.' Jane straightened up and broke away from Buck's embrace, calmer now. She stepped through the garden gate of the lodging-house and turned to face him. 'I guess I should thank you. Well, I'm very grateful, Buck. Thank you for stopping him.'

'You gonna be OK?'

'Yes, I think so.'

28

'Good girl. Try to git some sleep. No need to thank me, unless' – he grinned at her – 'you'd like to give me a goodnight kiss.'

Jane shook her head, smiling at him. 'You never stop trying, do you?'

'You missed all the fun.' Snake Stevens strolled into the dining-room of the Grand Junction hotel and ensconced himself at the Rudges' table, putting his boots up on a spare chair. 'Some great oaf of a hill-billy snatched the Merriman gal.'

'Jane Merriman?' Rachel Rudge was a wiry, pert-faced girl. Sparks of jealousy flashed in her glassy green eyes as she pronounced her rival's name. 'Is she OK?'

'Sure. That rodeo rider, Bradley, rescued her. He roped the big, hairy bear, near choked the life outa him. The fella looked like he'd been livin' in the woods for years. He claims he wants the gal as his squaw. He was lucky he wasn't lynched. The sheriff's lodged him in the pokey.'

'You don't say?' Robert Rudge mused. 'Well, my dears, Snake and I have some business to discuss so perhaps you would like to go take the air out on the veranda?' A big, bluff man, formally attired in a grey suit, a diamond stickpin in his cravat, Rudge ushered his females out, and slumped back in his chair. 'A pity whoever he was didn't make a proper job of it. That would have solved my problems.'

'What problems?' Snake helped himself to brandy from a cut-glass decanter. The Junction was where big ranchers, dealers, railroadmen and oil-strikers gathered to talk business and provided nothing but the best. 'You in need of my services?'

'Yes.' Rudge lowered his voice and glanced around the half-empty dining-room. 'I want that Merriman gal and her horse outa the rodeo. The same goes for Buck Bradley.'

'You mean you want them out, like dead?'

'Killing may be too strong a solution. I'm not planning on standing on a scaffold.' Robert Rudge scraped fingernails across his balding dome, trying to cover the deficiencies with what hairs remained. He had a neatly clipped beard to compensate. 'All you have to do is make sure those two don't get to the finals in Oklahoma City, no way. Break their legs. Get rid of their horses. Do whatever you have to do.'

Snake took his lucky silver dollar from his pocket and spun it in the air, catching it again. It had once saved his life when he was on the receiving end of a heart shot down in San Antonio. He had kept it in his breast pocket ever since. 'Maybe that bozo in jail could do this for us? Sure, he was brimful of rotgut whiskey, but he vowed to get Bradley and take the gal as his squaw. He's a man of the feud. All I got to do is grease the sheriff's palm to get him released, then stir the great bear up, remind him of what he's gotta do.'

'Right. They'll be going back to their ranch. It's down in the Ouachita forest some place. Maybe that would be the perfect spot? Well out of the way. I don't want anybody connecting me to this. I'm leaving it up to you. You've always taken care of things nicely for me before.'

'Yeah, well that was yesterday. Today is today. My overheads have increased.' Snake spun the coin again and gave his shifty grin. 'This Bradley ain't some ordinary Joe. He's in the limelight. There could be a lot of comeback. I already got the federals looking into my activities. If a guy like this gets lead poisoning they're gonna sniff a rat. The same goes for the gal. And her damn hoss, too, come to that. Breaking legs is no good. Best to zero them all. Maybe I can get Ebenezer Johnson, Junior, to do the dirty work. But if he messes up it's gonna be down to me and my boys. So I'm gonna be needing a thousand each, man, gal and hosses. That's three thousand green uns.'

'You're joking?'

'No, I never joke about money, nor about killin' people. I take my work seriously, Mr Rudge, and it don't come cheap. Hell, ain't I heard you've just capped a new gusher? It'll be fillin' your barrels with black gold. You're a rich man, Rudge. You can afford me. Three thousand, or no deal.'

'It's daylight robbery.' Rudge's face hardened as he lit a cigar and glowered at the gunslinger. But it was too late now to get anyone else and Snake Stevens was reputed to be the best. 'A thousand for getting rid of a couple of horses? You're crazy. Still, I guess you're right. We'll have to kill them all. Dead men, or women, come to that, tell no tales.'

'Just outa interest,' Snake drawled. 'What you got against Bradley?'

'I got big money riding on Dusty. And I don't like the looks that cocky cowboy gives my wife.'

'Don't you trust your lady?' Snake gave his thin-lipped sneer and stroked his pencil moustache.

'It ain't that, but you know these wimmin, they go weak at the knees over rodeo riders. She keeps talkin' about his successes, rilin' me. The trouble is we've got more servants than we need and she's got sweet Fanny Adams to do. I ain't got the time to keep an eye on her. So Bradley's gotta be chopped.'

'Count it done. If Ebenezer don't cut out his guts, I'll force him into a gunfight' – Snake gave a cackle – 'preferably when his back's turned.'

'All right, three thousand it is. But I don't want anyone pointing the finger at me. If anything goes wrong you're on your own. Come to my office at The Roost in the morning. You'll get half down, half on completion. We'll celebrate at the finals in Oklahoma City.'

'We sure will, Rudge.' Snake got to his feet. 'Shall we join the ladies?'

'No. The less I'm seen with you the better it will be. You can be on your way.'

'Right. Have the money ready tomorrow.'

Rudge watched the gunman saunter out of the hotel. 'Yech!' He spat cigar juice at the spittoon. 'What a way to earn a living. He gives me the creeps, that guy.'

Three

Jane Merriman lunged out of her nightmare with a choking scream and sat up in bed in a cold sweat. 'What's wrong, honey?' Sally Sago, in the bed beside her, was awoken, startled. She put an arm around the girl. 'Are you OK?'

'It was him. That brute with the beard. He was trying to get me.'

'Hey, now. It was only a bad dream. He's safely locked up. You gotta forget him.'

Jane's luxuriant black hair fell in a tangle over her face as she clutched her nightdress to her and stared into her memories of the evening before, revivified by the awful dream of him getting his hands on her again. 'It was him. He won't give up. He swore he was going to have me as his squaw and he meant it.'

'Don't be ridiculous.' Sally, with rags tied in her curly hair, patted her shoulder, tried to soothe her. 'Dese are the 1890s. Modern law-abiding times. A man cain't go round doin' dat no more.'

'You don't know' – the girl gave a sob – 'what a crazed brute like that can do.'

'Sho', I know. I'm a Nigra ain' I? Before yo' daddy took me in I seen plenny bad things what white men

33

can do. But, that fella, he's as dim as a hog. He won't remember you. Look' – she pointed out of the window at the dawn's first light – 'dat ole sun's comin' up once more. Rise an' shine, honey. We gotta get Snow Storm ready to load on the railroad. Train leaves at ten o'clock. Less go see if dere's any cawfee stirrin'.'

'Yes.' Jane shook her head as if to rid herself of the images. 'It was only a nightmare. I'm OK now. Go see if you can get any hot water for bathing.'

She was looking forward with a sense of relief to returning for a while to the peace and safety of her her father's ranch to prepare for the finals at Oklahoma City

'It will be good to be home,' she murmured to herself, as she rose from the bed, although, as she did so, a shiver of cold – or was it a fearful premonition – made her shudder. 'What's the matter with me? I'm behaving like a frightened girl.'

Yes, she had been shaken by the events of the night before, but she could cope. She had to be sensible, put it all behind her, concentrate on her performance and the care of Snow Storm. He was the finest horse she had ever schooled. And powerful: he could leap a five-barred gate almost from a standing start. She was convinced he was going to be a champion. Jane was proud of the fact that for the first time in her life she was earning money. Not just the small-time prizes of her home county affairs. No, there was big money to be made at the territorial finals. Her father would be proud of her. The cash would go towards the upkeep and improvement of their horse ranch. He hadn't had it easy since his accident. Now she could do something to help. Clint Merriman, come to think of it, hadn't had it easy since his wife died of a fever when Jane was only ten and he had struggled to run the ranch, compete in rodeos, and raise his daughter on his own.

It had been a lonesome life for a girl, without any sisters and brothers, until one day he had returned, when Jane was fourteen, with the thirteen-year-old Sally. He had rescued her from a children's reformatory. She had, apparently, had a terrible life, unschooled, abandoned, running wild, abused by men, insolent, resentful. Using patience, understanding and firm kindness, Merriman had gradually won the girl around. It had been intended she would be employed as a 'help' on the ranch, but she had become more like one of the family.

Jane was smoothing out her showdress on the bed, and choosing clean underwear when Sally came puffing up the steep stairs with two bowls of milky coffee on a tray. Behind her a boy was struggling with two pails of steaming water. He tipped it into the small stirrup bath. As Jane went behind a screen and stripped off her nightdress, Sally called to her, 'You take first dip.' She pressed a dime into the boy's hand and clipped him behind his ear. 'OK, sonny, off wid yo'. Yo' needn't think yo's stayin' here to watch.'

Ebenezer Johnson, Jnr., cocked an eye open beneath a shaggy brow as he heard voices out in the jailhouse office. He groaned and put a hand to his pounding head as he lay sprawled on the bunk. A hammering whiskey hangover was no big deal, but today, as he tried to shout out to whoever it was, he could only raise a croak. He felt like a horse had kicked him in the throat.

'Waal, how d'ya feel, man?' A dude in snazzy black clothes was standing looking at him through the bars. 'A little the worse for wear?'

'What's it to do with you, ratface?' The mountain man forced the words out through his bruised oesophagus. 'What am I doin' in here? You the sheriff or somebody?'

'No, I'm just a friend, a well-wisher, you might say.' Snake Stevens' cadaverous face forced itself into a phoney smile, even though the stink of the hairy giant made him want to grimace and recoil. 'The sheriff's allowed me to have a few words with you.'

'Yeah?' The bunk groaned as Johnson swung his huge weight around to sit up, and scratched, perplexedly, at the hair around his throat. 'What the hell's happened to my voice? I can hardly talk.'

'Don'cha remember? That bastard stomped on your windpipe.'

'No, not much. Only some kinda ruckus. Who was he?'

'The rodeo rider, Buck Bradley. You swore to kill him, Ebenezer. In front of all those folks you swore to have vengeance. He took your gal from you.'

'Gal? What gal? What you talkin' 'bout. My head's spinnin'. Why don't you go git me a cawfee?'

'I'll have a pot sent over. Don't you remember her, Ebeneezer? The tall, slim gal with the long black hair? She was wearin' a straw sombrero.'

'Aw, yeah. I 'member.' The big man's pink lips pouted as he blinked out of all his hair. He looked morose. 'She was boo'ful.'

'She sure was,' Snake drawled. 'She sure still is. A real humdinger, eh, boy? Don'cha remember sayin' you was goin' to take her as your squaw. What Eb'nezer Johnson wants, Eb'nezer Johnson has, just like his liver-chawin' granpappy.'

'Aw, piss off, squitface. You think I'm stoopid? You think I'm gonna admit to doin' somethang? Go shit yourself.'

'I ain't tryin' to trick you, Ebenezer. I admire a big man like you. A real man with big guts.' Snake grinned at his own remark for Johnson certainly did have a girth on him. 'I got news for you, boy. That gal, she wants to see you agin. She had to pretend to be averse to you because that fella Bradley's sniffin' after her. But she's a friend of mine, an she tol' me she wants to see you agin. She's had enough of small-fry. She wants a real man, a big man like you, someone who treats her mean, someone who can satisfy her. She's all woman, boy, and you're the lucky man she's wantin'. How you do it, Johnson? What you got that I ain't?'

The great, bloated giant lurched to his feet and caught hold of the bars, his face straining as he tried to bend them apart, but they were embedded deep in the rock, and solid. 'You tryin' to be funny, smartass?' he croaked out. 'I get outa here I'll tear your heart out.'

'Simmer down, Eb'nezer. Would I lie to you? That's more than I dare. Here.' Snake reached in his shirt pocket and pulled out a rodeo programme, tapping a finger at the Ladies' Horse Trials events. 'There's her name and picture. Jane Merriman. Took first prize. They got where she lives written down there. The Lazy River ranch, Big Cedar. It's down south the terri'try, way out in the forest, but easy enough to find.'

Liver-eating Johnson, Jnr., snatched the programme from him and stared at it. It was just a blur to him. 'That right? That where she lives?'

The great, ignorant cretin, Snake thought. He can't read, can he? 'Her place is easy enough to find, pal. Head south on the railroad to Hugo. Buy yourself a hoss at Broken Bow and go east to Big Cedar. Just ask for the Merriman ranch. Everybody knows her. They'll point you on the way. You can keep that programme, just show it to folks. I've underlined her name.'

'Yeah?' Johnson's vicious little eyes studied the gunman, puzzled. 'What's in it for you? Why you doin' this?'

'Nuthin's in it for me, Johnson. What you think I am? I admire your frontier spirit, thassall. And last night, after the fracas, Jane told me how she feels about you, asked me to pass the message on. She's got the crazy hots for you, boy. She wants to see you again. But the trouble is Bradley's got a hold on her. He thinks he's a big shot, thinks he can boss her around. He's nobody, only a cowpoke on her old man's ranch. He's taking her back there today. The trouble is he's been braggin' that if he sees hide or hair of you near that place he'll kill you, shoot you dead.'

'Yeah? That pisspot cowboy? Who's he think he is? I ain't sceered of him.'

'Of course you ain't, Eb'nezer, but you got to go stealthily. Bradley near kilt you last night, stompin'

38

on your throat like that. We had to pull him off. He don't fight fair, jumped you from behind.'

'Yuh.' Johnson stared intently at the programme, at the little inset picture of Jane. 'I 'member now. Thass her, ain' it?'

'Yeah, thass your squaw. Cute, ain't she? If you take my advice' – Snake lowered his voice – 'you'll kill Bradley 'fore he can kill you. Then grab the squaw under cover of darkness. Head east into Arkansas. Don't worry about her daddy. He's a cripple. He cain't come after you. But maybe you better kill him, too, while you're there. Thass my advice I'm jest offerin' as a friend.'

'Yuh?' The giant man scratched his hairy chest beneath his rags. 'But how do I git outa here?'

'You'll be out tomorrow. The judge is a friend of a friend of mine. Here' – Snake took twenty dollars in bills from his pocket and slipped it to him – 'he'll fine you two dollars for bein' drunk and disorderly. Don't go spendin' the rest on whiskey. It'll pay for your ticket to Hugo and on to Broken Bow. Then you can buy a ten dollar hoss and git after her.'

'Yuh? But I still don't see why you—'

'OK, I see I cain't fool a man like you – I'll level with you, Johnson. Bradley ain't no friend of mine, either. You'd be doin' me a favour if you put him outa the way. Here, you better have another ten for expenses.'

'Mister' – the mountain man gripped the cash in his paw and beamed at Snake – 'you got yourself a deal.'

'Good,' Snake drawled, and winked. 'Have fun with your new squaw, you lucky damn sonuvagun.'

He stepped outside the jailhouse and nodded to the town sheriff who was sat in his rocker on the sidewalk. He was on Rudge's payroll, too. 'See you, Matt.' He stuffed a cheroot, with a note wrapped around it into his shirt pocket, 'Take it easy now.'

The Kansas and Texas Railroad, known more familiarly as the KT, or 'Katie', headed south across Oklahoma Territory connecting those northern and southern states and making defunct the need for the long cattle trails of the not-far-distant past. On its single track the sturdy little 'Katie' engine was idly steaming, taking on water and wood ready for the long haul down towards the Texas border.

Buck Bradley, with his loose-hipped rodeo rider's swagger, was leading Red Desert along the line of wagons, his boots crunching on the gravel, when he saw Jane Merriman at the top of a ramp let down from one of the box cars. She was leaning forward trying to push her horse, Snow Storm, back into his stall. The stallion, for his part, didn't seem to appreciate the comforts of riding in style and was protesting shrilly. Jane, in a plain cotton workdress revealing sun-tanned calves in beaded moccasins, was hard-pressed to keep the stallion in, calling out, 'Stay, boy, stay!'

Buck gave a low whistle through his teeth. 'She sure got a tasty rump, ain't she?' he muttered.

Jane managed to secure the stallion in his box and began backing away down the ramp, but suddenly slipped on some fresh dung and would have gone flying had not Buck leaped in and neatly caught her in his arms, breaking what might have been a nasty fall.

'Whoops!' He scooped her to him tight, one hand around her back, the other beneath her *derrière.* 'Careful, sweetheart.'

Jane swallowed her squawk of alarm and met his mischievous eyes in his bronzed, laughter-lined face. Too late to avoid the kiss he placed on her nose. 'All right,' she said. 'You can put me down.'

'Is that all the thanks I get? What you gonna do when I ain't around to look after you, Janey?'

'Come on, Buck. We gotta get the ramp up. The darkness will calm him. Hurry! He might make a break.'

'Yep.' Buck knew better than to fool around where a stallion was concerned. He swung her lightly down and together they raised the ramp and locked its bolts into place.

'Waal, there y'are.' Buck grinned at her. 'All we gotta do now is git Red Desert and Reno's hoss on and we'll be ready to go. Where's Sally?'

'I don't know,' Jane said. 'She was supposed to be helping me. What are those three doing here?'

She nodded over in the direction of Snake Stevens, Ace Weston and Danny McCafferty, who were leaned against the shiplap wall of the booking office in the shade of its canopy, watching them. Snake in his shiny black leathers and low-crowned hat, grinned wolfishly as he met their regard, and spun his lucky silver coin in the air. There was something deeply malevolent about the threesome.

'Beats me. Two of 'em's card-sharps, ain't they? Mebbe they're jest headin' down to the Tishomingo festival to cheat a few of the Indians of their beads?'

'I don't like the look of them.'

41

'It's a free country.' The whistle was blowing, steam shooting from 'Katie's' tall stack. 'Come on. Time to git aboard.'

They got their other horses into a wagon, hurried along the track and climbed into one of the passenger cars. Reno stood outside. 'Where's Sally got to?' he asked.

The stationmaster was looking at his watch, raising his green flag, the guard walking along, slamming doors shut. 'Come on,' he said to Reno. 'You getting on or not?'

'Wait a few minutes,' Jane pleaded, looking out of the door window. 'We can't go without—'

'We got a timetable to stick to,' the guard grumbled, as Reno climbed into a further door and the train began to move away, shunting out smoke, its bell clanging, wheels grating on the lines.

'We gotta stay with the hosses,' Buck said, but suddenly spied the maid running as fast as her legs would go in the restraints of her tight skirt. Her bosom beneath her blouse was bobbing violently with the motion. 'Come on, gal. Run!'

Sally ran on alongside the moving train, puffing and panting, her eyes wide, her cheeks glowing. 'Got ya,' Reno shouted, as he grabbed her wrist and hauled her in.

They all gathered in seats facing each other, Buck and Jane side by side opposite Reno and Sally, who, after she had caught her breath, explained, 'I been along to see the sheriff. I tol' him that lunatic oughta be locked up for life.'

'So,' Buck asked, 'what did he say?'

'That depends on the judge. Thass all he'd tell me.'

'Maybe we shoulda stayed,' Reno suggested, 'an' given evidence against him. My cut arm, fer instance.'

Jane shook her head, vehemently. 'I just want to get away from that place.'

She tried to pull herself away from Bradley. His arm against hers as they rocked up and down to the motion of the train was too close for comfort. She looked across at Reno, squat and muscular, in his fringed leathers and battered boots, a knife in his belt. He was a cheerful sort, a headband around his brow to keep his coarse hair from falling across his face, which looked like a horse had kicked it in. Well, he couldn't help that. But why was Sally tucking her arm into his and snuggling up to him? There was no future in it. He was another rolling stone, like his pal, Bradley. Both drifters. All they thought about was riding bulls and wild broncos, getting rip-roaring drunk in some saloon. Skirt-chasers and trouble makers. Jane didn't wish to be a prude but Sally had hinted she had survived in her wild, childhood days by doing men sexual favours. Surely she ought to see the folly of such ways?

'Don't you two cowboys ever plan on settling down?' she suddenly blurted out. 'I mean, you can't go on like you do for ever.'

'Hey, Janey.' Buck grinned, turning to her, his arms stuck out. 'Are you proposin' to me?'

'Don't be absurd.' She turned her head away to watch the great clouds of smoke rolling by across the sun-bleached prairie aware of a flush of embarrassment creeping into her cheeks as his regard bored into her. 'Can't you have a sensible conversation? Do

43

you have to make a joke of everything? Anyhow' –
she gave a huff of indignation – 'why should any girl
want to marry a man like you?'

'Huh. A man like me?' Buck slumped back in his
seat. 'You sure know how to put a fella down.'

Jane stared out at the sere prairie which seemed to
stretch away limitless, at the telegraph wires following the railroad line, seeming to rise and fall, hypnot-
ically. She ignored him, closed her eyes, tried to
sleep.

Sally Sago popped her eyes, made a face at Buck,
and tried not to giggle. If Jane Merriman wasn't
happy, she certainly was.

Buck flicked a wink at her. He tipped his hat over
his nose. 'Yeah, I guess we could all do with some
shut-eye.'

Four

It was a long haul jogging across the prairie, the line running straight as an arrow until they crossed the Canadian River, spanned by a trestle bridge. Then the country became forested and hilly, the engineer in the Katie engine 'Whoo-whooing' his steam whistle to scare game, elk and deer, off the line as they wound through gorges and crossed ravines. On and on they went, way across the territory, stopping and starting, until night began to fall. Jane passed around a picnic supper she had prepared, potato omelettes, slices of ham, hunks of bread, which they washed down with the only beverage available, luke warm water from their canteens. Occasionally they would stretch their legs and walk down the cars to the viewing platforms for a breath of air. As it grew dark they settled down to sleep. The train was no longer crowded and the four friends found empty seats so they could stretch out their legs. They should be in Hugo by the morning.

'OK, boys,' Snake Stevens hissed, gently poking Ace and McCafferty with his silver-toed boot to wake them. 'It's time for us to go.' It was in the early hours of the morning. They had chosen seats at the back of a carriage closest to the boxcars. Nobody noticed as they roused themselves to leave.

The Katie was slapping on its brakes, wheels locking, carriages clanking and groaning, as they eased to a halt to take on wood and water somewhere in the south of the territory. Most folk merely surfaced for a few seconds to try to make out where they were, then went back to sleep. But it would not be unusual for one or two to get out and jump down onto the track to take a look at what was going on, which is what Stevens and his men did. They were alone in the wooded night, apart from the engineer and fireman by the engine calling out to each other as they went about their duties.

'Come on.' Snake led the way, crunching back along the track on the gravel bed past the box cars containing all manner of goods and parcels, until they reached the specially constructed horse box with its let-down side. It was the last wagon before the conductor's caboose.

'Do your bit,' Snake told McCafferty, who had once worked on a railroad and knew how to uncouple vans. 'Give him a hand, Ace.' They had picked their spot fortunately for they were on a downwards slope and wouldn't need the engine to back up to loosen the couplings. They had brought a slegehammer along specially for this job and Snake listened to the tell-tale chonks, the grating and clanking sounds as he strode on back to the conductor's van.

'What's going on?' A uniformed man stepped out of the van door, a shotgun in his hands, which he levelled at the figure approaching along the track.

'Beats me,' Snake replied. 'Two of your railroad boys seem to be doing a bit of repair work. I've come along to tell you I want to get my horse out at the next halt.'

'What horse?' The conductor eyed the thin-faced man in his leather coat and pants and silver-toed boots, keeping him covered with the twelve gauge.

'You know, the stallion. Them other four is just my employees.'

'First I heard of it,' the conductor remarked, but he made the mistake of jumping down onto the track to go along to investigate. As he did so, Snake caught the shotgun barrel with his left grip, pushing it to one side, and socked the guard hard to the jaw with his right fist. The railroadman went down on one knee but hung onto his shotgun. Snake drew his revolver and buffaloed the conductor across the jaw, poleaxeing him.

As he collapsed, he gave him another across the back of the head to make sure. He relieved the prostrate man of his peaked hat and green flag and went along to his companions.

'You finished?' he snapped.

'Sure,' McCafferty grinned. 'Dese horses won't be going nowhere. At least, not wid dis train.'

'Good.' Snake heard a halooing shout from along at the engine as it got up steam ready to move. He put on the cap, stepped out into the moonlight, and waved his flag. 'Nuthin' to it, is there?'

'Hail,' Ace croaked, smacking his palm across Snake's in triumph as they watched the train go bobbing away into the night. 'We done it. Them

47

dimwits is goin' to get a surprise when they git to Hugo in the marnin'.'

'Now, let's see,' Snake drawled, 'all we gotta do is get this boxcar ramp down and unload these precious animals.'

That wasn't going to be as easy as they imagined. The big stallion, Snow Storm, was not used to rough handling by strangers and began shrilly whinnying and refusing to budge. Snake hit him across the face with his fist which made him curl his lips back and try to bite him, screaming his anger. It took the three of them to haul him down the ramp to the ground.

Snow Storm was by no means finished. When Snake tried to saddle him, he whirled around going up on his backlegs, flailing out with his deadly shoes. Ace hung on grimly to his head-harness as the horse kicked and reared, instinctively fighting these men, trying to make a break for the wilds. It wasn't until McCafferty slipped a rope around a back leg and tied him to a tree, holding him, painfully, on three legs that they had him tamed and ready, and, as the Irishman slipped the rope, Snake swung on board. It was, for a few minutes, like a scene from the rodeo, as Snow Storm bucked and kicked, trying to rid this man from his back. But Snake had a Westerner's way with horses, if a brutal one, as he held him firm with a cruel spade bit, and gradually calmed him down.

'That's got the bastard. Right, you ready with them other two?'

Red Desert, infected by Snow Storm's shenanigans, or sensing something amiss, was also a problem to mount, whirling away from Ace, until he was whipped into submission. The powerful quarter horse was unused to such treatment, or to another man on his back, but Ace's vicious Mexican spurs showed him who was boss.

Reno's piebald, Magic, was more docile and McCafferty had little problem climbing onto his back.

They were about to pull out when the middle-aged conductor came to his senses, groaning at the bump at the back of his head. He should have played doggo, but instead, as he groped hold of his shotgun, he swung it up and shouted, 'Hold it. Stay where y'are.'

Snake Stevens' Remington was out in double-quick time, raised like a snake about to strike. And, as the conductor squeezed the shotgun trigger, the revolver cracked out, the bullet piercing his chest, making him fall back in agony, the shotgun's pellets spraying the bushes, harmlessly.

The conductor groaned, clutching at blood spilling from his uniform. Snake fired another slug, and he fell back, his agony over.

Stevens spun the revolver and slipped it back in his belt holster. 'Damn fool. He asked for it. Come on, let's git moving.'

'Where we goin'?' McCafferty shouted, as he followed the rump of the spotted Appaloosa.

'South to the Red River,' Snake called as he hung onto the powerful stallion. 'There's a man I know down in Texas who'll pay top price for these animals. So, we're gonna have to take it easy on 'em. Keep 'em in good shape.'

'That Appaloosa is priceless.' Clint Merriman was seething with anger. He had been waiting at Hugo

49

railroad depot. When he saw the Katie engine box and guard's van, he had made his way painfully over to them on crutches. 'I'm holding the railroad responsible.'

'Livestock is carried at the owners' risk,' the Hugo station master replied hastily. 'I'm sorry about this, Mr Merriman, but those is the regulations.'

'That horse ain't no ordinary animal. I'm talking in thousands of dollars here, his basic price, his potential for prize money and at stud. If he ain't found, I'll sue. You shoulda taken better care of him.'

'You shoulda taken out your own insurance on him, Mr Merriman. I ain't got time to argue. I gotta send an engine an' crew back to see what's happened to the conductor and his van. He mighta come uncoupled by accident. The damn horses might be sittin' there safe and sound for all we know.'

'I doubt that very much,' Buck Bradley muttered, anxiously glancing at Jane, who appeared to be on the verge of tears. 'Vans don't git uncoupled by 'emselves.'

'All this talk of dollars,' she cried. 'Please, don't! Snow Storm's worth more than dollars to me. He's my horse. I've put my heart into training him. What we've got to do is find him. I'm so frightened. He may be ill-treated. Or killed.'

'I don't think they would do that,' Merriman consoled her. 'That would be foolish. He is too valuable a horse.'

'These things happen, Dad. Whoever's got him might just want him dead, just to keep us out of the contest.'

'No, they could easily have pizened him, not go to

50

this trouble,' Buck said. 'I'm just as worried as you, Jane. Red's a valuable rodeo hoss. They might be wanting me outa the finals, too.'

'Yes, I'm sorry. You feel the same as me. What are we going to do?'

It had not been until daylight that the engineer had realized the caboose and horse box were missing. Instead of making a two-hour trip back to the last water tower stop, it had been decided to go on into Hugo to report the loss and to deliver the rest of the passengers and cargo on schedule.

'I'm gonna go see the sheriff, try to raise a posse,' Clint Merriman said. 'We'll send out a search party. They won't get away.'

'I ain't so sure of that,' Buck mused. 'They coulda gone north, south, east or west, any point of the compass. There's only seven hundred thousand folks live in this vast territory. Searchin' for three hosses is going to be a tough proposition.'

'We'll go back, pick up their tracks.'

'Thass gonna take one hell of a time, Mr Merriman, even if you do raise much of a posse around here.'

He meant that Hugo was no longer a typical Western town of cattlemen and cowboys. It had become the centre of the circus industry, where troupes congregated to assemble and train performers before heading out on tour.

'The only posse you gonna raise,' Reno opined, 'is strong men, freaks and dwarfs.'

'So,' Merriman snapped, 'what do you suggest?'

'Well, to start with, we ain't got no hosses now, so we're gonna have to find fresh mounts.'

'That's no problem,' Merriman said. 'We brought in a dozen of our spare hosses with us to sell. They're along at the corral. They ain't top quality plugs, but they're good enough. Help yourselves.'

'Right, Reno and me'll go after 'em.'

'I'm coming with you,' Jane said, eagerly. 'You can't stop me.'

'Oh, yes, we can,' Buck replied. 'If we catch up there could well be gunplay. This ain't gal's work.'

'He's right, Jane,' Merriman said. 'I'm not letting you go.'

'Havin' to pertect you would only hinder us,' Buck pointed out. 'Now, le's see, which way they likeliest to have gone? Hardly back north towards Tulsa. The hosses are known in those parts. East across the border into Arkansas? I don't think so. It's too rugged and mountainous, too many rivers to cross.'

'Waal, there ain't much point them goin' west,' Reno put in. 'There's only a scattering of ranchers, farmers and the tribes out there. Where would *they* raise the cash for the price them hosses are worth?'

'So, we can't be sure, they coulda gone any which-ways. But my guess is south. Texas is as rodeo crazy these days as are the folks in this territ'ry. There's plenty ranchers down there with big money to spend.' Buck got down on his haunches and scrawled a rough map in the dust. 'Thass the Red River, the border with Texas to the south. I was raised along the valley. There's only certain safe crossing points. I figure we should check them out, pick up their trail, or maybe even get there before them.'

' 'Course,' Reno said, 'they could try to get to El

52

Paso, cross over into Mexico, sell 'em to some rich *haciendado.*'

'Nope. I don't think so. Those ain't long distance horses. Mine's built for speed over short distances, same as Reno's. And Jane's, well' – he grinned at Reno – 'he ain't much more than a pampered rodeo hoss.'

'Rubbish,' Jane protested. 'He's got amazing strength and stamina.'

'Maybe, but there ain't much point in 'em frazzling them valuable nags. I figure Texas.' Still balanced on his haunches, he poked at his map. 'Nearest big town due south is Dallas, but they could be making for Wichita Falls or Fort Worth over here to the west, or, maybe as far south as Waco. Hell, who knows, they could be headin' for some spot, unknown to us, where they can unload this hot property. Our hosses ain't well known in Texas so they would be easier to show, or sell on.'

'Oh, God,' Jane moaned, clutching her head, 'I can't stand it. Poor Snow; who knows how he'll end up?'

'Come on, Jane, bear up.' Merriman put out an arm to grip his daughter's hand. 'Buck's got the right idea. All us noncombatants can do is wait and hope.'

'Yes,' she whispered, 'and pray.'

'I want that hairy bear Johnson, let out of jail as quick as you can, Harry,' Robert Rudge shouted as he burst into Judge Vygold's office.

Harry Vygold frowned, shook his head adorned with greasy black curls, and indicated a portly, middle-aged man sitting in a chair beside his desk.

'This is Marshal Sam Gray visiting out of Fort Smith.' He introduced the men. 'Robert Rudge, our leading citizen.'

'Yes, I've heard of him.' Gray did not stand to shake Rudge's proffered hand. 'Why you so interested in having Johnson released, Rudge? From what I've heard he merits a two-year stretch.'

'No.' Rudge gave a nervous, scoffing laugh. 'It was only a drunken brawl. Nobody was hurt.'

'He tried to abduct a respectable young girl with a knife to her throat,' the judge pointed out. 'Not exactly a drunken brawl, Bob.'

Gray looked like his name: a head of white hair hanging over his brow, parted to one side, a heavy grey moustache, and attired in a three-piece tweed suit of the same sober hue. 'I asked what's your interest in getting Johnson out?'

Rudge was ruffled. He had not expected to find a lawman in the judge's office. Sam Gray had a solid reputation as a defender of justice and was not likely to be a man who could be bought. 'I just think it would be best to run a man like that out of town as quickly as possible. Why should we pay for his upkeep?' He sought wildly for some other excuse for his request. 'Also, the girl he messed about with has left town. I understand she would not want to testify against him. Nor do I think we should force her to undergo such an ordeal.'

'Hrrmmph.' Gray sounded doubtful. 'Well, for a start, I ain't a marshal. He's back at Fort Smith sat on his butt doin' the paperwork. I'm one of his several deputy marshals out in the field.'

'A well-known and respected one,' the judge said.

'We are prepared to give you every help. Sam is looking into the activities of Snake Stevens, Bob. Wasn't he an employee of yours for a while?'

'Yes, he was, in a way.' Rudge felt even more rattled, so took time out to light a cigar and ensconce himself in an armchair. 'I used him for security purposes in my business, the saloon and the oilfields. He did a good job keeping troublemakers out.'

'I bet he did.' Sam Gray permitted himself a brief smile and hitched up the bulky shoulder holster under his coat. 'How many men did you have him kill?'

'What? That's outrageous. None of course.'

'Really? How about a man called Rachsweitch?'

'He was a troublemaker, tried to organize a strike. Stevens shot him, but it was in self-defence.'

'I could mention other names, recently deceased. No doubt you would say they were all fair fights?'

'How do I know? All I know is Snake is fast and accurate. You get a reputation like that as a gunman, others seek you out. Unfortunately none, from what I've heard, have been fast enough.'

'Or, fortunately, for Stevens. OK, I give you I don't have much solid evidence against Stevens, but that's what I'm here for, to take a look at his activities. I'd appreciate the help of you gentlemen.'

'Of course.' Rudge was a little too rapid with his support. 'If Stevens has broken the law then he should be apprehended.'

'As should be the men who use his services?'

'If they use them for unlawful purposes, yes,' Rudge agreed hurriedly. 'But, if you're having a dig at me, Mr Gray, then I can only say I see nothing wrong in employing a man to protect my property and business premises.'

'No, why not? You get trouble with your business rivals or workers, you bring in the heavy mob, is that it?'

'Judge, do I have to sit here and be insulted?'

'The marshal – deputy marshal – is not insulting you, Bob, he's just making enquiries.'

Judge Vygold squirmed under both men's regard. He was not exactly on Rudge's payroll, but when he was not on the bench he ran a prosperous dry goods store in the town and he needed the considerable business put his way by Rudge and his oil-field employees. On the other hand he had to make it appear to the authorities at Fort Smith that he was dispensing justice in a proper manner.

'I'm inclined to agree with Mr Rudge here, Sam, that what this drunkard Johnson needs is a short, sharp sentence. Possibly a month's hard labour, don't you think?'

'Well, I guess that's better than kissin' his backside and tellin' him not to do it again.'

Rudge sighed. 'Personally, I'm looking forward to the day the Dawes Commission completes its report and Oklahoma is put forward for statehood. Maybe then we can run our own affairs, not be dictated to by the Arkansas judiciary.'

'Yes, but until that day we're still in charge of things.' Gray replied. 'And don't you forget it. So, you any idea where I can find Stevens?'

'None whatsoever.' Rudge rose to leave. 'I'm a busy man. If there's nothing else I can help you with I'll be on my way. Time is money, as they say. Good luck, Marshal. So long, Harry. Yes, a month sounds fair enough.'

The deputy marshal waited for Rudge to depart, then muttered, 'Why's he so anxious to have Johnson on the loose. I don't trust that fella. I'd like to know what he's playing at.'

'Aw, you've got a suspicious mind, Sam. S'pose it goes with your job. But I can assure you Robert Rudge is highly respected in these parts. Without him this town wouldn't be what it is.'

'Maybe.' Sam Gray got to his feet to leave, too. 'So, he's a bigshot, but that don't give him carte blanche to bend the law to suit himself. A few people around hereabouts had better start cleaning up their act and you' – he pointed a finger at Vygold – 'ain't no exception, Judge.'

Five

Buck Bradley and Reno rode their mustangs along the meandering Red River in a westerly direction keeping a sharp look-out for hoof-prints, but travellers were few and far between in these parts and the only tracks they saw were of unshod ponies ridden by the natives of the Choctaw nation.

'Maybe they gone east along to Colbert's Ferry,' Reno said. 'Maybe we're on a wild goose chase?'

'It's possible. But I'm gamblin' they chose the easier route across the grasslands. Don't start gettin' maybe on me.'

They travelled light, packing beef jerky, hard tack biscuits and a bag of flour in their saddle-bags. Buck's old .52 calibre seven-shot Spencer carbine, stuck through the saddle cinch under his knee, was his heaviest equipment. Reno carried a Colt handgun, with a bow and quiver of arrows across his back, the latter useful for shooting game without a gunshot giving away their location. A couple of grouse he had bagged dangled from his saddle horn.

'It's good to see the ole Red again, ain't it?' Buck looked across the wide but shallow stream, its low banks liberally covered with salt cedars. 'But where in tarnation they goin' to try to cross?'

Even to a native of the area it was always tricky crossing the Red with its shifting banks of treacherous quicksands. Hundreds of cattle being herded across had sunk out of sight in those long reddish stretches of sand that gave the Red River its name.

They rode all day until the sun began to bleed away and they reached the old steamboat landing at Cotton. The log buildings of this out-of-the-way spot had fallen into disrepair, deserted and ghostly, a loose shutter banging in the wind. Once the Choctaws would have shipped their bales of cotton downstream, but now they humped them to the nearest railroad depot.

'This was where I was raised.' Buck stepped down, and poked into the main cabin. All that remained were a couple of broken chairs on its dirt floor by a stone fireplace. 'Home sweet home.'

Reno built a fire in the grate and set to plucking the grouse and roasting them, while Buck crushed coffee beans with his gun butt and boiled up big, black, tarry mugfuls. 'Them birds sure smell sweeter than jerky,' he said, as he lay back resting against his saddle.

When they had filled their bellies, he pulled out a small bag of Bull Durham and rolled cigarettes. 'My daddy spent most his days cutting cordwood for the steamboats. Us boys helped him. Then the steamboats ceased comin' and it looked like our livelihood was gone. My Pa got into an argument with a drunken 'breed, Cherokee Dan, you remember him?'

'What happened to him?'

'He got himself shot dead. A year later Ma passed

away. Died of heartbreak, I reckon. They were good people. They never did nobody no harm. We kids were in our early teens. Two sisters got wed and went to live down in Texas. My two brothers headed for Wyoming to raise cattle. I followed the rodeo, an' I been followin' it ever since.'

Buck drifted off to sleep, his carbine between his knees while Reno took first watch. After midnight, Reno woke him tossing more wood on the fire and Buck roused himself to let the part-Comanche get some sleep.

For two days they prowled along the banks of the Red River rarely seeing a soul, but, if they did, questioning the passing Indian or trapper as to whether they had seen three men on distinctive mounts, one spotted, one chestnut, the third piebald. All they received was a dumb shake of the head.

When they returned to Cotton they saw the telltale hoof-prints in the wet sand. 'Shoot!' Buck gave a whistle of disgust. 'I had a feelin' we shoulda hung about here.'

'Them's day-old prints.' Reno studied the deep shoe marks of the heavy horses. 'See the ant tracks across 'em? I'd say them three crossed over last night. At least we know now where they are.'

'Yup. Only hope they made it. Not that I wish them fellas well. Don't want 'em drowning the hosses. Come on, let's git after 'em.'

It wasn't just quicksands they had to be careful of. There was always the danger of being bitten by poisonous snakes, the water moccasin, that lurked in the waters. Buck cut a willow branch and poked at any dangerous-looking sandbars as they gingerly rode their mustangs across.

From then on, although it was early fall and the ground was baked hard, it was easy enough for a part-Indian like Reno to follow the trail. 'Ole Magic looks like he lost a shoe. They gonna have to stop at a town someplace.'

It was bleak, flat country, the ground turned to dust in places due to overgrazing by longhorns. Sure enough the trail led to a ramshackle small town, named Good Fortune, and a livery.

'Sure.' A burly blacksmith eased his back to look at them. 'Them three passed through yesterday on fine-looking horses. I charged 'em three dollars for shoe-ing the patch. I gotta make an extra dollar outa strangers, ain't I?'

'Any idea where they were headin'?'

'Yeah, they asked how far to Fort Worth.'

'What's all the hullabaloo down the end of the street?'

'Aw, they're lynchin' a Nigra. He molested a white gal. When they put a hot poker to him he confessed.'

When they rode along to take a look, a young black was kicking his last hanging from a telegraph pole, a host of ragged, dusty folk, men, women, kids, sullenly staring at a photographer under his black sheet recording the moment for posterity.

'These Texans don't mess about,' Reno said. 'It sure weren't good fortune here for that boy.'

'Nope.' Buck spat in the dust. 'Let's git outa here. This scene's giving me a bad taste in the mouth.'

They followed the wind-eroded and sun-blasted lanscape, an oppressive heat making their shirts cling to the sweat on their backs, until they reached the Brazos River.

Fort Worth had once been a stockaded army post on the edge of the western frontier. For forty years the word Comanche had been synonymous with terror. But the land had been wrested from the hands of the 'savages' and Fort Worth had become a populous and prosperous community. The town was *en fête*, bunting strung across the main street, the sidewalks crowded with people. And from the corrals outside town came sudden roars of applause.

'Hey!' Buck's sunburned, unshaven features cracked into a grin. 'Looks like we've arrived in time for the rodeo.'

But they had more serious matters on their minds. They tethered their broncos by a water butt, and Buck, carbine in hand pushed into a saloon called The Golden Horseshoe. It was practically deserted. Everybody was along at the rodeo. They slaked their own thirsts with flagons of iced beer and asked the bar-keep if he had seen the three desperadoes. 'One of 'em's a shifty-eyed, rat-faced galoot, thin as a rake, in black leathers.'

'Them, yuh. They was in. On a lucky winnin' streak. They gone along to the hoss sales.'

The horse sales. Maybe they were too late?

'Come on,' Buck hissed, not waiting to finish his drink. 'We might be in time.'

What few folks were about stared at them as they jogged down the main dusty drag towards the arena: the cowboy, a carbine in his hands, in his flapping batwing chaps, the half-Comanche in fringed buck-skins and headband, a bow and quiver on his back.

They pushed through the crowds around the main arena, standing six deep, hooting and hollering as a bunch of Texans tried to catch and saddle a herd of wild mustangs, hanging on around their necks as the critters bucked and screeched defiance.

To one side was a corral where up on a raised podium an auctioneer was rattling out his half-comprehensible spiel. 'Hai-yeer we have Snow Mountain and Red Cloud, two stablemates, won most the prizes in the Oklahoma champeen-ships. They're offered for sale jointly. Who will start me at two thousand dollars?'

Buck shoved through the wealthy ranchers hanging over the rails and saw Ace Weston and Danny McCafferty parading Snow Storm and Red Desert around the ring. He searched the faces but there was no sign of Snake Stevens.

'Just a minute,' he shouted, as he vaulted the rails and landed on the toes of his high-heeled boots. 'These horses ain't theirn to sell. They belong to my boss and me.'

The auctioneer, gavel in hand, stopped in his tracks. 'What in hell you talkin' about stranger?'

'I'm sayin' those two are dirty, lowdown, hoss thieves. An' there's another of the snakes about somewhere. They oughta be strung up.'

'What de blazes is de man talkin' about?' McCafferty protested, as he hung onto Red Deseet. 'We bought dese horses fair and square.'

'Thass right,' Ace shouted. 'They're ourn. That man's got a crazy grudge. It's him who should be locked up.'

'That's my hoss and I can prove it.' Buck gave a

piercing whistle between his teeth. 'Come here, Red.'

The quarter horse's eyes bulged at the familiar command and he reared up, whipping his reins out of McCafferty's hand, and cantering over to Buck, his head held high.

'It sure looks like your horse,' the auctioneer began as men started muttering agreement.

'You lousy, lyin' bastard.' Weston whipped his gun out and took a fast pot at Buck beneath Snow Storm's neck. The Appaloosa shied from the explosion and broke away. Ace backed away, too, fanning the hammer of his six-gun. 'Take that,' he shouted.

Buck ducked to one side from the whanging bullets. He jacked a shell into his Spencer carbine. He hit Ace square on, knocking him back off his feet.

'Sonuvabitch!' the cardsharp gasped as he lay in blood and dust.

McCafferty hauled his heavy handgun from his belt, finger around the trigger and aimed a shot at Buck. Reno was sat half-over the rail; his bow, arrow poised, string tautened back to his jaw. The arrow pierce McCafferty's throat, going in the front and sticking out the back. He went down coughing blood.

Suddenly Snake Stevens appeared behind Reno. He swung his revolver felling the Comanche with the impact of its butt to the back of his head. It sounded like the crack of a coconut. Snake spun the revolver back into his hand. And fired.

Buck instinctively stepped to one side as the slug whistled past his head. He levered another shell into the carbine and aimed at Snake. The powerful .52 calibre bullet smashed through the corral rail showering splinters.

Snake Stevens carefully raised his revolver with the mechanical exactitude of a professional gunslinger and squeezed out another shot. Buck tried to fire the carbine from the hip again and ducked. This time he wasn't fast enough. Snake's bullet scorched against his temple, knocking him spinning backwards, his head cracking against a gate post, and he rolled unconscious.

Either Snake thought he was dead, or he didn't wish to wait and argue with the angry onlookers, one of whom had been hit in the leg and was screaming vengeance. He took one look around at the four bodies sprawled on the ground, turned and pushed hurriedly away through the crowd. He unhitched an unattended mustang, hurled himself into the saddle, and galloped out of town, his coat tails flying. Revolvers blammed as men fired wildly after him, their bullets whistling past his head, but he rode on, flaying the horse with the reins, until he had disappeared from sight.

A bucket of water in the face brought Buck spluttering to his senses. 'Whass happened? Am I still alive?' The brawny town sheriff was kneeling, peering at him. 'Yeah, I must be. There couldn't be nobody ugly as you up in heaven.'

'A smart-mouth huh?' The pink porcine fellow stared at him, unblinking. 'You got any proof them hosses are yourn?'

'Yep.' Buck sat up and leaned against the shattered corral post, looking across to see Reno being revived. 'They ain't mine. Belong to my boss, Clint Merriman, of the Lazy River Ranch up in Choctaw country.' He pulled a crumpled piece of paper from his shirt pocket. 'Here's their credentials, registration as thoroughbreds.'

Pigface peered at the paper. 'Sure, I heard of Merriman, rodeo rider from way back. Still alive is he? Heard he'd been hurt bad.'

'Yeah, he can hardly walk, but he's OK, still running his ranch.' Buck got to his feet, picking up his hat and carbine, brushing himself down. 'Red Desert used to be mine, but I got broke. Gored by a damn bull. So Merriman bought him from me and finances me to compete. We go halves on the prize money.'

'You a rodeo rider?'

'Sure I am, what in tarnation do I look like? But, enough chit-chat. What in hell's happened to Snake?'

'Aw, he took off. Looks like he's headed south on the trail to Waco. I never did like the looks of that *hombre* since he hit town.'

'Aincha goin' after him?'

'Nah. Too hot. He's well away. We got a rodeo goin', boy. I'm needed to keep an eye on Fort Worth. Doncha worry. We'll git him. I've telegraphed his description down to Waco.'

'Right. You can tell 'em he murdered a conductor on the K an' T, up near Antlers when he stole these thoro'breds.'

Reno was groggily rubbing a bump on the back of his head, as he wandered across. 'We goin' after him, Buck?'

'No, the sheriff here's takin' care of things. We got the horses back. Thass all that counts. I don't figure we'll see much more of that snake Snake.'

'C'mon, boys.' The sheriff slapped them on their backs. 'I'll buy ya a beer in The Horseshoe. Best saloon in town. You look like you could do with some treatment to that bullet crease on your temple, mister.'

'Aw, I'm OK.' Buck, suddenly dizzy, grabbed the rail. 'Yeah, I guess I could use a beer.' He glanced across at a top-hatted undertaker busy measuring the corpses of Ace and McCafferty. 'Looks like the burial fees are down to me, eh?'

'That's usually the case, my friend.' The sheriff gave a belly- laugh. 'An' you'll have to pay the doctor bills of the man who got a bullet through his leg. Then we might let you go.'

Reno went across and pulled his arrow from the throat of McCafferty, wiping the blood from its iron point. 'Hm,' he grunted. 'Nice edge on it, huh?'

'Yessuh, Comanch'. Neat shootin',' the sheriff boomed in his deep voice. 'I'm kinda glad we ain't still at war.'

'OK,' the Tulsa town sheriff growled, unlocking Ebenezer Johnson, Jnr's, cell. 'The Judge has sentenced you to a month's hard labour and that's what it's gonna be. You've got some stones to break.'

Johnson raised his gross weight from his bunk, his bloodshot eyes blinking from the hairy morass of his head. He thumbed at his whiskey-red pitted nose and lurched out, awkwardly, in his leg-irons and chains. He was barefoot in ragged trousers, his great flabby biceps protruding from a vest that had long since seen better days. 'All right mister, I ain't gonna cause you no trouble.'

The sheriff carefully covered him with his shot-gun. 'I certainly hope not, Johnson, or there's gonna be one big hole in your grizzly gut.'

He leaned over to close the cell door, but as he did so Liver-eating Johnson, Jnr., twisted the carbine from his grasp, put a brawny arm around his throat, and with the other lifted him under the crotch hurl-ing the none-too-slim lawman crashing against the barred gate. Then he bludgeoned him with the carbine now in his own paw. 'Listen hard, Sheriff. Nobody tells me what I gotta do.'

The sheriff's eyes bulged in his blood-streaked face as the carbine pressed hard across his throat and Johnson kneed him in the groin. 'No – ahhgh!' He made a croaking sound as his windpipe was crushed and he slumped to the ground.

Johnson knelt on him until he was sure he was dead. He took the sheriff's keys, unlocked his irons, found his boots and his bear-pelt coat. 'Like takin' candy off a baby,' he said, with a gappy grin, picked up the shotgun, and, locking the office behind him, sauntered away down the dusty street. At this time of the morning the town was practically deserted, most men out at the oilfields or their farms. At the railroad depot it so happened a train to Hugo was just pulling out, so he bought a ticket and clambered aboard. 'So long, suckers,' he growled.

Six

Buck woke in the hay of the livery stall beside his horse. His head was pounding and it wasn't only the fault of the bullet crease across his temple. The bottle of rotgut whiskey they had downed might have helped. Fort Worth was packed to the seams for the rodeo. People had flocked in from far and wide for what they called their national finals. There had been no chance of getting a bed in a hotel. Still it was better than sleeping out among the snakes and scorpions infesting the rocks along the Red River.

'We're low on funds,' he muttered to Reno who was watering his piebald, Magic, glad to have him back. 'These thieving Texans charge enough for coffins and doctoring. An' we musta got through a pile last night. Who *were* those gals?'

'Aw, jest a gaggle of Texan chickadees. They seemed to think we was made of gold.'

'Yeah, lucky they didn't have the shirts off our backs.'

'Yuh know,' Reno said, 'I'm gittin' mighty tired of these chisellin' goodtime gals. To tell the truth I'd kinda like to settle down with Sally Sago.'

'Hey, man, I nevuh thought I'd hear you say such a thing,' Buck drawled, stroking his unshaven jaw. 'But to tell you the truth I'm kinda worried about Jane. I guess we'd better be gettin' back.'

'Say pal, listen to the famous Buck Bradley.' Reno gave a grin of mirth. 'The original tumblin' tumbleweed. The guy who boasted no filly would ever rope him.'

'It ain't that. Anyway,' he muttered, darkly, 'she don't want me. It's jest that I'm worried about her safety.'

'Me, too, pardner. So, what shall we do, sell them other two mustangs and ride?'

'Hey, hold on, not so fast. First I wanna get me some breakfast, a shave and a bath in the barber shop. And, well, it's the last day of rodeo, the pony races. Maybe we can take these loudmouth Texans for a dollar or two?'

'Maybe we could.'

But that was easier said than done. The Texans played to win, even if it meant using every cheating trick in the trade. In the mile race, once they were out of sight of the crowd, they would whip their opponents in the face, or try to run them into the rails. Reno could only make fourth place.

When it came to the quarter-horse races Buck on Red Desert should have been able to lead the field. His copper-coloured quarter horse was a muscular bulldog type with well-rounded hind-quarters and a deep heart. He was part-thoroughbred with a terrific acceleration, like most of his breed, which makes them ideal for roping cattle or cutting a cow out of a herd. Buck had carefully bred and nurtured him

70

from a foal, but his recent cruel treatment under Ace Weston's whip and spurs had made Red Desert nervous.

As they gathered at the starting line most of the Texans began whipping their horses to a frenzy so they would blast away at the 'off' like bullets from a gun.

'Hey, I ain't ruining Red like that,' he called to Reno, as he walked Red around behind the others, 'Look, man, can you ride Magic down the track for a bit?'

The ruse worked. Red Desert's ears pricked up as he spotted his stable mate heading off and he was eager, when the flag came down, to spring off to join her. Buck kept him going alongside the whooping Texans but all the whipping and screaming seemed to unnerve his horse and he only managed to get in third although he hardly seemed to draw breath over the fast quarter-mile.

'Heck,' Buck said, after he had collected his meagre prize money, and they turned their mounts' heads back towards the north. 'I've had enough of Texans and Texas. They can keep it. Let's go home.' Home, after all, it occurred to him, is where the heart is.

Reno raised an eyebrow. 'Home?'

'Yeah, a man needs a place somewhere to hang his hat.'

Liver-eating Johnson, Jnr., clambered down from the railroad car at Hugo and stood perplexed, staring, like an awed child at a string of elephants being watered nearby. 'Hell,' he said, 'they're bigger than me.'

He lumbered up the main street, feeling like he might be in a dream as men on stilts, clowns in harlequin garb, acrobats and girls on tightropes practised their stuff, apart from the yapping poodles and barking seals with balls spinning on their noses. Ebenezer was unaware that this was the circus capital of the West. It was all kinda crazy.

He had tossed the sheriff's shotgun away. What he needed was a repeater. There might be trouble at his squaw's ranch, wherever the hell it was her daddy had her hidden. Well, her daddy wouldn't worry him as long as he had the right armoury and ammunition.

He grabbed hold of a passing dwarf and hoisted him aloft. 'Hoy! How do I git to the Ooh-ah-cheetah forest?'

'How the hell do I know?' The dwarf struggled and squealed, indignantly. 'Go ask at the railroad. You probably got to take another line.'

Johnson let him drop, unceremoniously, and sauntered until he spied a gunshop. The bell clanged as he ducked his head and pushed inside. The proprietor looked up at the bearded giant of a man. 'Yessuh, how can I help you? You with the circus?'

'No, I ain't. Do I look as if I am? Listen, pintsize, I want the best carbine you got. I mean business.'

'Ah, yes, sir, in that case I would recommend a Volcanic. Here we are. You see, it has an attachable steel stock, you can use it either as a handgun or with a shoulder-rest for greater accuracy. I'll throw in a box of slugs; it's yours for fifty dollars.'

'Yuh,' Johnson grunted. 'This ain't a bad idea, I can hide it under my coat, like. Where can I try it out?'

'In my back room, sir. I've had it specially converted for practice.' He led the big man out into a covered yard with a wooden dummy at one end among sandbags. 'It's loaded, just pump the trigger lever.'

'Yuh.' Johnson held the Volcanic to his hip, blasted away at the dummy. As the powder smoke cleared he muttered, 'Yuh, thass purty good. Fifty dollars, yuh say?'

'Yes, sir.' The little, bald-headed owner went up to the dummy. 'Good shooting, sir. Every one on target. Ten of them. Where's the other two? Did you spend them?'

'No,' Johnson grinned. 'I'm savin' them for you, you idjit.' He jerked the trigger, viciously, and the gunshop owner hurtled back, hanging onto his dummy, sliding down as blood trickled from his chest.

Johnson turned on his heel, found the box of slugs, rifled the till, and left the shop. 'Served him right, tryin' to cheat me.'

At the depot, a train was just leaving for Broken Bow. 'That's your best stop for the forest trail,' the guard told him. 'Goin' hunting'?'

'Yeah, I sure am,' Johnson growled.

As he lay back and watched the woods flowing by, he muttered, '*Woman* hunting. That squaw won't git away from me so easy.'

Snake Stevens finished his bacon rashers, grits, and eggs over easy in a Waco diner, ran a fingernail through his moustache and picked at his teeth, as the waitress poured him another black coffee. He felt secure, although shocked: Ace and that idiot McCafferty dead? Sure, it was OK to kill someone you didn't know, but having one of your own, or two, in this case, stunned a man. What to do? He'd got an easy $1,500 down payment from Rudge. Why not clear out, head down to Mexico, let things cool? But his conscience prickled: he was a professional. He was renowned for finishing a job. If you've been paid for a job you had to see it through. 'We shoulda killed those damn horses,' he muttered. 'That was a bad mistake. I got too greedy. And I underestimated that Bradley guy. I won't make the same mistake next time.'

Whether to return to the fray, or whether to call it a day? He idly picked up the the *Waco Daily Newshound* and glanced at its front page. Then sat up straight, his hair prickling beneath the brilliantine. 'Gunfight at Fort Worth Corral,' the headline read. 'Two horse thieves dead.'

With a start his eyes registered the daguerrotype likeness on the right hand side of the story. It was a mirror image of himself. 'Snake Stevens, the man behind the daring theft of two championship horses and believed to be the killer of a railroad guard, is on the run in Texas. He was last seen headed for Waco.'

Snake's throat constricted as he read the damning evidence and description. His eyes darted about the restaurant but they all appeared to be a load of dumb Texans stuffing themselves for the day to come. 'Shee-it.' He slid his plate away, tossed down a few dollars. 'I gotta get outa here.'

Across the way was a haberdashers. He flicked his beloved flat-topped hat, with its hatband of rattler skin, onto one of the piles of rubbish that lined the street, and stepped inside. 'Gimme one of them dusters,' he said.

He pulled the long canvas dust-cheater over his leathers, and tugged a ten-gallon Texan hat over his ears. He hadn't shaved in a while and his moustache was no longer much of a pencil, but beginning to grow like his beard. Soon the flourishing hair would join up with his sideburns. What better disguise in a land of hairy men?

'I'm gonna finish this,' he said, as he climbed on his mustang. 'I got two people and two horses to kill.'

Normally, Jane Merriman's heart would have swelled to see her homeland, McCurtain County, again with its vast green forests and crystal-clear waters, more than one and a quarter million acres of mountains, ridges, rivers and lakes. They went clicketing along the single track through the Ouachita Forest, which meant Happy Hunting Ground, and that was what it had been to her since childhood. But today she gazed despondently out of the train window, her thoughts full of premonitions of danger and loss.

'Cheer up, sweetheart.' Her father, on the opposite seat, leaned forward to pat her knee. 'Buck and Reno are fine young fellows. They'll get the horses back. Won't they, Sally?'

'They sho are, and I sho hope so, Mr Merriman, suh,' Sally smiled. 'We nearly at Broken Bow, ain't we?'

It was the end of the subsidiary line which was mainly used by lumber men to haul trees out of the forest. The locomotive came to a gasping, clanging halt, and Clint clambered down painfully on his crutches. He had been a rodeo rider most of his adult life. He had had his share of tragedy, his wife dying, then the horse falling on him, and had probably left it too late to retire from the arena, but rodeo was in his blood. It pained him to see his daughter struggling to put a brave face on the loss of Snow Storm and all their hopes of breeding a champion. 'Come on, let's get the rig and horse and go home.'

Soon they were jogging east along the track into the forest, sighting numerous bear, the hillsides mantled with oak and pine, the shinier green of mistletoe entwined in the branches, the leaves of the maples and beech showing as patches of red and gold in the early fall. It was a long drive and they fell silent as the sun began to set, warming their backs. They followed the winding course of the fast-flowing Kiamichi River, looking across to the blue folds of the mountains to the south, and cast off north to Big Cedar, with its sawmill and, as its name implied, an ancient cedar tree which towered 125ft. tall. They called hello to the sawyer and his family and took the trail to Beaver Lake.

It was nearly dark by the time the two-horse buggy reached the gateway to the Lazy River Ranch and they saw lanterns burning in the windows of the white-painted clapboard house, with its white turret, standing on its hill amid pastures of grazing horses and cattle.

'Home!' Jane cried, with a sigh. 'It's always so wonderfully peaceful.'

She was not to know that it would not stay that way for long.

76

*

In the morning, Jane took a look at the other Appaloosas she was schooling. They were one of the world's oldest breeds, pride of ancient rulers, and favoured war mount of the Nez Percé Indians. Like snow flakes, no two Appaloosa coat patterns are alike. Snow Storm was one of the finest examples of the breed, deep through the chest and girth, with a quiet eye and noble temperament. She would, she knew, never find one like him again. But there were several mares in the corral and another of her favourites, Waltzing Boy, gave a whinny of recognition and galloped over to her. He was a skittish three-year-old, but she had high hopes of him.

The ranch foreman, Black Hawk, a Choctaw, came over to lean on the corral rail beside her. He had heard of the loss of Snow Storm, but in his silent, dignified manner made no mention of it, simply, somehow, communicating his sympathy. Instead, he pointed to a sorrel a farmer had brought in, claiming he was 'evil' and unmanageable.

'We got to sort out his trouble, Jane. I been settlin' him in.'

'You've always told me there's no such thing as an evil horse, Hawk. There's just ill-used or badly broken ones. A little kindness and understanding should fix him.'

'I told the farmer we wouldn't charge him unless we cured him, 'cept for his feed. You know what he said?' – Hawk gave her a grin – ' "If so, you're the first honest horse dealers I ever met".'

'That's probably why we never make much profit,' she said. 'But at least folks know we're good for our word, eh, Hawk?'

'They sure do, missy. They come from far and wide to see us.' It was he, and her father, who had taught her, since the age of three when she had her first pony, all she knew about horses. It was Hawk, too, who had brought them their first Appaloosas and started their herd. Nowadays, with her father in a wheelchair, Hawk more or less ran the ranch. 'Waal, I gotta get the boys movin' and out on the range,' he said. 'You take it easy today, Jane.'

He was a good man. His wife, or squaw, was similarly hard-working, and Jane waved to her as she went across to the barn to milk the cows and feed the chickens. In many ways theirs, in this secluded backwater, was an idyllic life. Why should it all suddenly start to fall apart?

They are beautiful horses, the Appaloosas, Jane thought, as she watched them gracefully grazing or cantering about. The Nez Percé had been a handsome peace-loving people, too. But in 1877 settlers had caused trouble and, in the ensuing war, the great Chief Joseph led his tribe on a 1,300 mile march through the Rocky Mountains, fighting off the US Army all the way, until he was stopped thirty miles south of the Canadian border. The tribe had been relocated to the Nations, but they did not settle well and in '85 most had been removed to a reservation in the State of Washington. Before that, however, Black Hawk had purchased the nucleus of the Merrimans' herd for them.

Jane spent the morning seeing to things about the ranch and taking a look at the sorrel. He was in a bad way. In the afternoon, she and Sally took a ride out to

Beaver Lake to watch these busy creatures building their log dams and lodges. They managed to coax some up to them. Like any animal, if offered affection they responded with trust.

The glass-still lake and dark, silent conifers, however, filled her with gloom, and when she returned she could not shake off a sense of apprehension . . . .

Ebenezer Johnson had used the gunsmith's money from his till to buy a sturdy cart-horse, with feathered hooves, who would easily carry his weight, rather than one of those knock-kneed mustangs most men rode. He left Broken Bow and headed at a steady rolling lope into the Ouachita forest. Luckily, what few folks he met had heard of the Merrimans and pointed him on his way. He passed through Big Cedar and reined in when he reached a sawmill. The sawyer offered him refreshment and he stuffed himself, ill-manneredly, at their expense, making loud eructations both 'fore and aft, as the sawyer's wife and daughter watched him, wide-eyed.

Johnson picked his broken teeth with a blackened fingernail and growled, 'How far to the Lazy River ranch?'

'Not far. Ten miles up the trail,' the sawyer said. 'You a friend of theirn?'

'I got business with 'em.' The huge, bearded stranger cleared his throat, spitting on the floor.

'Hoss business?'

'Yuh, thass it. How many men they keep there?'

'There's her daddy, only he ain't much use these days, and Black Hawk, the Choctaw ranch foreman, an' two other boys. Why?'

'I jes' wondered, thassall,' Johnson muttered,

darkly.

'Thass a hefty piece,' the sawyer remarked, looking at the big Volcanic with its hickory birdclaw butt, brass magazine, and twelve-inch barrel.

'Yeah, this is a fifty-dollar gun. Man needs pertection in these woods, don't he?' He picked it up and turned it on them. 'I thank you folks for the grub.' His little pink mouth with the broken teeth opened in a grin. 'That fooled ya, didn't it? Ya thought I was goin' to blast ya to smithereens? Nah, I ain't like that.' He lumbered to his feet and pulled on his bearskin coat. 'I'll be on my way.'

He stuck out a grimy finger at the frightened family. 'Anybody arsks, you know nuthin' 'bout me. You ain' even see'd me. You remember that or I'm likely to be callin' in on my way back.'

He climbed with some difficulty onto the big horse and set off on his way again. Dusk was closing in by the time he reached the gates of the ranch and saw the white wooden house with its pointed turret, up on the slope. There was fenced-in pastureland all around. No way of getting up there without being seen. He would wait until dark.

Seven

Jane used a curry comb on Waltzing Boy to remove the mud from the boggy lake, and, as a misty dusk moved in, walked him across to the corral.

'Thass her,' Ebenezer Johnson hissed, as he gloated over her tall, lithe curves. 'Thass the black-haired bitch. Thass my squaw.'

Up at the house a middle-aged man, tall and rangy, too, had hopped out on crutches to sit in a basket chair on the veranda. He was lighting a pipe as he was joined by a redskin of similar years, in range clothes, but with a feather in his hat. He, too, lit a pipe.

'That must be her daddy,' Johnson muttered, as he watched from the shadow of the pine trees. 'An' thass the Choctaw foreman.'

Jane walked up to stand on the veranda talking to them and presently, two scruffy ranch hands strolled across from the barns. Sally came to the corner of the house from the kitchen where she had been helping Hawk's squaw with the cooking, clanged an iron triangle, grinned at them and yelled, 'Come an' git it.'

'Thass the black gal who hit me with her brolly. I

81

got a bone to pick with her. Right, thass the whole
damn brood. They'll be gittin' their noses in the
trough. Here's my chance.'

Ebenezer hitched his cart-horse to a tree and,
breathing hard, half-ran up the hill. In his thick fur
coat and half-crouched posture he looked part-man,
part-bear in the gloom. The Volcanic dangled from
his right fist.

He reached the stables without being spotted and
paused, panting for breath. The moon had yet to rise
but he could see through the half-darkness the slant-
ing trapdoor of a storm shelter beneath the veranda.
Maybe he could hide in there?

But, first, he needed to take another look at the
girl. He gallomphed across the yard in his heavy
boots and crept, as quietly as he could, up steps to
the veranda. He tiptoed along the creaking boards to
an open window lit by lamplight, through which a
curtain billowed. He caught it, held it open a crack,
and squinted through.

Yeah, there they all were, sat around a table having
supper. A dumpy squaw brought in trays laden with
food. The black gal was chattering. Jane Merriman
smiled as she passed soda bread rolls around to the
men. For moments, it seemed to Ebenezer she was
smiling straight at him. That fella was right, he
thought, she's here, waiting for me.

All he had to do was deal with her daddy. He was a
cripple so he wouldn't be any problem. The Choctaw
looked like he might be handy with a knife. And he
could see the other two had sidearms holstered to
their belts. So what! Just dumb ranch hands.

Two big, tan-coloured 'coon hounds were sitting

by the table begging for scraps. As Johnson opened the curtain a fraction and strained to hear what was being said, one of them scented him and padded across towards him, growling. He suddenly leapt up, his forepaws on the sill, and began barking frenziedly. Ebenezer retreated along the veranda, the boards thudding under him. He half-tripped down the steps, recovered himself, and scuttled along the side of the house.

Black Hawk leaned out of the open window and saw a big hairy shape going towards the barn. 'It's a durn grizzly,' he yelled, and fired his scattergun after it.

Ebenezer gave a blood-curdling scream, jumping and hopping as buckshot buzzed about him. He ran into the barn and, in the light shed from the house, saw a ladder leading to the hayloft. He clambered up it. 'So, they want to play like that, do they?' he growled.

'Let the dogs out, Steve,' Clint Merriman snapped at one of his ranch hands.

But Johnson had come prepared for dogs. He had lumps of lard in his pocket, laced with strychnine like the wolf-hunters used. He heard the hounds howling as they raced towards him, leaned from the loft and called, 'Hello, nice doggies.' When he dropped lard down to them they began gulping it up. 'Here y'are, eat your supper.' Ebenezer tossed them two more lumps. 'Sweet dreams.'

As Steve, the ranch hand, walked stealthily towards the barn he called to the dogs fearing they might be ripped to pieces by a cornered grizzly. 'Where are you, boys?'

The heavy dose of strychnine was fast-acting. One of the hounds was already having convulsions and the other was trying to regurgitate the lard as the ranch hand reached them. 'What the hell's going on?'

'Guess?' Johnson jumped from the loft and landed on his back. He caught hold of Steve's hair, slit his throat with his razor-sharp Bowie, cutting on down his sternum and ripping his abdomen apart. 'My grandaddy'll be proud of me,' he gurgled as he opened the man up and cut out his liver.

'It's gone mighty quiet,' Clint Merriman said, as he propelled his wheelchair out onto the veranda. 'Steve!' he shouted. 'What's happening?'

'I'll go take a look,' Black Hawk said.

He ran towards the barn and the two girls followed him. Black Hawk had the shotgun in his hands and Jane an oil lantern. 'Oh, my God!' She spoke in a hushed voice as she saw the disembowelled ranch hand. 'It's *him*!'

'Who's him?' Black Hawk asked, as he peered up at the loft.

'It couldn't be. He's locked up miles away.' Sally Sago gave a shrill squawk of fear when she saw the writhing dogs. 'Look at them poor thangs.'

'It's him.' Jane trembled, her face distraught. 'It must be. He's come to get me.'

'Ain't nobody in the loft. Maybe he's round back of the house someplace.' Black Hawk's glistening eyes reflected their own horror and fear. 'I'll go take a look. You girls get back in the house quick. Bolt the doors, shutter the windows. This ain't right.'

When they were gone he prowled around the

house, peered across at the woods, and returned to the front. The storm shelter was unbolted. He levered a shell into the shotgun, keeping it in his right fist, his finger on the trigger, as he hoisted the wooden doors apart. 'All right, mister,' he shouted, 'I know you're in there.'

Down in the dark cellar Ebenezer Johnson had hidden his bulk behind a pile of old furniture, resting his Volcanic on top of a battered chest of drawers. He tried not to breathe as he heard the Choctaw calling out, and saw his shadowy shape stepping down into the cellar. The Indian had a spooked look in his eyes as he kicked logs aside and swept the carbine in an arc. 'Where are you, you varmint?'

Johnson squeezed the trigger of the Volcanic and Black Hawk was catapulted by the force of the big slug back onto a pile of logs. 'Where the hell you think I am, dimwit?' He put another bullet into the Indian to finish him, the noise of the explosion ringing in his ears. 'I ain't got time to butcher you, but I'll be back.'

Inside the house, the girls frantically finished barricading the lower windows and doors. 'What's that?' Sally screamed as there was a muffled roar from the cellar below them.

But Black Hawk's squaw knew what it was and as she squatted on the floor, began rocking back and forth emitting an agonized moaning death chant.

'For Chris'sakes shut her up,' the other ranch hand, Randy, shouted, his cocked revolver ready in his hand.

'Jane, get up stairs, lock yourself in your room.' Clint Merriman sat in his wheelchair at the foot of

the stairs, watching the front door. 'And you, Sally.'
He had a Winchester carbine in his hands. His gaunt-
jawed face was set firm. But he sounded rattled.
'Randy, be ready to shoot to kill. Take no chances.'

'Yooouh.' Randy peeped through a gunport in the
shutter. 'But, Mr Merriman, you heard what he did to
Steve, to them dogs. Why should a man do that? He
can't be human.'

'He's tryin' to scare us. We've got to stand firm,
Randy. He's only a man of flesh and blood. There's
one of him, two of us. We can take him.'

For the first time in her life Jane Merriman regretted
not learning to shoot a gun. Her father had discour-
aged her. There were not many armaments in the
house, for he always claimed that too many guns
caused accidents. And, anyway, this backwater had
been a haven of peace for many years. She went to
peer out of the window. The moon was beginning its
rise, shining silvery blue on the barn roof and she
could see the horses over in the corrals. There was no
sign of the intruder.

'Oh, my God,' she whispered, clutching her arms
to her, staring at Sally as they cowered in their
bedroom. 'I can't stand this.'

'Take it easy, Jane. Your Dad and Randy can deal
with it. They'll go for the Choctaw police in the
mornin'. They'll get him.'

'The morning's a long way away,' Jane whispered.

Ebenezer grinned, gripping his Bowie in his teeth,
his Volcanic in one massive hand, as he climbed the
hayloft ladder to the window where he could see a

86

candle flame flickering. He manoeuvred one fat knee onto the windowsill, caught hold of the sash with his left land and didn't hesitate, hurling himself through.

Jane screamed as the huge bear of a man came crashing through the glass, thudded on the floor-boards and rolled towards her. He caught hold of her ankle and hauled her off her feet. 'Gotcha!' he growled, as he lumbered up over her. 'Aincha pleased to see me?'

Sally ran into the attack, a jug raised in her fist. It smashed over his head. Johnson shook the bits from him, a tad dazed, and muttered, 'That ain't no way to greet me.' He swung the Volcanic with the full force of his massive arm, cracking the butt across the black girl's jaw. She tumbled to the floor, felled, blood trickling from her teeth.

Jane screamed and struggled, but he hauled her up before him, holding her tight in one arm, booted open the locked door, and charged outside. Randy was running up the staircase, his sixgun in his hand, but hesitated to shoot when he saw Jane. The Volcanic exploded flame and lead and Randy went tumbling back, cartwheeling down the staircase to lay inert.

Clint Merriman turned his wheelchair, but was unable to fire his Winchester as he stared with horror up the stairs and saw his daughter held as a shield before the brawny giant. The Volcanic spat flame again and Merriman felt the bullet tear into his side. He was propelled backwards in the wheelchair and tipped over into a corner. 'Oh, no,' he groaned.

Johnson half-carried Jane down the stairs, kicking

Randy's corpse out of his way. He aimed another slug at the fallen Merriman, but he was lying in his own blood, his eyes staring, and looked already dead. The bullet smashed plaster from the wall over him. He glanced at the moaning Choctaw squaw but decided she wasn't worth bothering about.

'Waal, looks like thass settled their hash, don't it? I ain't gonna eat their livers raw. I'm gonna fry 'em up for breakfast,' Johnson yelled. 'Me an' you, babe, we gonna make that bed bounce 'fore we git some shut-eye. Then we gonna have our breakfast and git outa here. You gonna be my squaw. You ain't never gonna git away from me, ain't no use you trying.'

Jane was frozen with fear, unable to speak as he turned his little piggy eyes on her, his pink lips in his matted beard opening as he pushed his hairy face upon hers, whining, 'C'mon, gal, gimme a li'l kiss.' His fingers pressed the back of her skull, forcing her face into him. Jane felt his wet lips sucking, desperately, at her own, as if he wanted to eat her.

She did the only thing she could think to do, bit hard into his pendulous lower lip, drawing blood. He jerked her head back by a handful of her hair, stared at her, his face clouded with hurt and anger. 'You wildcat. You're too fond of biting, you are. Thass gratitude, after I come all this way to git ya. I'm gonna have to knock some lovin' ways into ya, squaw. I'm gonna have to teach ya to obey.'

He released her hair and, fast for a big man, back-handed her back and forth across her face so that she collapsed back onto the stairs. 'Yeah.' He leaned over, breathing hard, and tore her dress apart as she half-lay there. 'Look at them nice li'l titties. I'm gonna be back for you. But, first I gotta git my knife. I left it upstairs. I gotta do some butchering.'

He glanced around to make sure that Merriman was out of action. His daughter had slumped limp as if drifting into unconsciousness, blood trickling from the corner of her mouth. Then, hanging onto the Volcanic he went stomping back up the stairs to the bedroom.

Merriman peered through his lids and hissed, 'Jane, you've gotta get out. Go!'

Jane stirred, dazed by the blows to her face. 'Dad, are you all right? You're bleeding; I can't leave you.' She put a hand out towards Randy's revolver on the floor. 'I—'

'No! Run now! I'll play dead. Get a horse. Go for help. It's the only way. Go on! Go!'

Jane stared at him, distraught, her hair hanging over her face. She got to her feet unsteadily, and staggered over to the front door. 'For God's sake, ride!' her father begged her.

The fresh air outside revived her, somewhat, and she ran over, barefoot, to the corral. There was no time to call to Waltzing Boy out in the pasture. She saw a rope hackamore hanging over the fence. She slipped through the rails, caught one of the frisky mustangs, quickly fixed the hackamore, opened the gate wide, jumped onto the mustang bareback, her legs astride, and herded the bunch before her out of the gate. 'Yah!' she yelled, as Johnson lurched out onto the veranda, raising the Volcanic, aiming at her. The mustangs did not hang about, what with the noise of the explosions and her urging them forward. They set off as one accord, streaming towards the open ranch gate at the foot of the slope. Jane ducked her head low as bullets whistled past her and she clung to the mustang's mane as he galloped away after the fleeing herd.

'The damn squaw. She gittin' away.' Johnson turned, perplexed, whether to stay and finish his grandaddy's work on the others? No, he had to get after her. 'She won't git far,' he shouted, as he went ambling away in his heavy bear fur down the hillside to look for his tethered horse. 'I'll ride her to hell. She won't git away from a Johnson.'

The mustang she was riding was barely broken. He had been on a lunge rein but he had yet to have a saddle on his back. Jane had difficulty controlling him with the rope hackamore, without a bit in his mouth. He was leaping and bucking and zig-zagging, thinking, What is this thing on my back; I've got to get it off! At the same time he was cantering along after the fleeing herd. Suddenly, he gave a leap that caught her unawares and she was flung forward, forced to hang on around his neck which sent him into a terrified gallop, his ears laid back. He sprinted on past the herd, and for moments she was among their whinnying and snorting and flying manes and hooves, and the next he was out in the lead. The girl was a natural horsewoman, but she could not regain her seat or slow him down. She just had to hang on for grim death and let him have his head. 'Oh, no,' she wailed as, instead of following the main trail towards the saw mill and Big Cedar, the mustang branched off along a narrower trail through the forest that led to Eagle Gulch and the falls. The girl was so dazed she could not hold him onto the proper trail.

However, after going for two miles at full pelt the mustang gradually slowed to a canter and then a trot and Jane sat upright and drew him in with the makeshift halter around his nose, soothing him. The mustang was sweating and trembling and, for that matter, so was she. Dawn was glimmering in the sky and she wondered what to do, whether to go on towards the river. But there were no homesteads she knew of in these parts. She might have to go for miles and miles before finding help. Should she go back? She sat there, her mind in a turmoil of indecision. Then, she suddenly heard the steady pounding of hooves. 'Quick!' she whispered to herself. 'We must hide.' But there was the start of a cliff to her left, and the boulder-strewn slope down to the fast running Kiamichi River to the right. And there he was, behind her, pounding along the trail on a big cart-horse. It was too late.

Startled, she swallowed her fear at the sight of the big, burly figure in his bearskin. She kicked bare heels into the mustang's sides, setting him off again. The little mustang, though, was tiring and blowing hard as they loped up a steep slope towards the clifftop overlooking Eagle Falls. The powerful, snaking, sheeny river was breaking into white water as it neared the rocks and surged over the 200-feet deep falls. She could hear it crashing and pounding into the whirlpools below. She whipped the mustang with the rope end. They were nearly at the top.

Johnson had fixed the iron stock to his Volcanic and held it tight into his shoulder like a carbine, squinting along the sights at the fleeing girl. Her mustang was slowing as it neared the top of the cliff.

Johnson had jerked the cart-horse to a halt. She was about a hundred yards away. Maybe with a lucky shot? He squeezed the trigger and smiled as the shot rapped out. 'Got her!'

All Jane knew was that she heard a shot clap out and her horse whinnied with agony as a bullet tore into his side. The mustang tumbled onto his collapsed forelegs to lie still. Jane was tossed over his head. She saw the edge of the cliff looming up, tried to slow herself, but went tumbling over its edge. The next she knew she was rolling and bouncing head-over-heels down the 45-degree slope until she finally came to a rest near the edge of the falls, bruised, bewildered, shaken, but not badly hurt. That, she feared, was yet to come. She was in terror of another beating, or God knew what, by this man. There seemed no way she could escape.

There was another clap of a carbine shot and a bullet spat past her hair. She looked up and saw him sitting on the big, powerful horse at the top of the cliff, watching her. He raised the carbine again, and, for moments she thought, this is it; this is the end, as he appeared to pull at the trigger. But nothing happened. He was out of lead! She scrambled to her feet again and set off along the river-bank, jumping from boulder to boulder, towards the falls, which were now roaring in her ears. She glanced back desperately and saw that he had left his horse and was climbing down the slope intent on cutting her off. In spite of his huge bulk, he was quite fast on his feet. She stared at her bearded pursuer like a petri-fied rabbit as he got closer and closer. It was her nightmare become fact.

Jane jerked her senses together, picked up a rock to defend herself, although she knew she had little chance against him, and set off again. Oh, no! She had reached the edge of the falls. She had run herself into a trap. There was no way she could go forward. She teetered on the edge, staring down giddily into the churning maelstrom of water and sharp-toothed black rocks. She shook her head. She could not jump into that! But what was the alternative? She turned and saw the bearded giant, grinning his puffy red lips at her as he got closer. He had the big Bowie knife in his hand.

Jane, her mouth dry with fear, tried to edge away but slipped and tripped on a jutting rock, cutting her leg. And it was too late, he was on her again, wielding the knife, twisting the rock from her hand, grabbing her by the hair, his vast sweaty, stinking body holding her down, his fetid breath in her face, as he gasped out, 'Too late, darlin', why ya runnin' from me? I tol' ya it weren't no use. Right, squaw, you've asked for it, an' this time you gonna get it.'

He ripped her dress further apart, thrust a knee between her thighs and clawed at her as she wriggled, fought and screamed. The falls rang in her ears, her head spun, as he stuck his knife in the sand, hauled her over onto a flat rock. He tore her pantalettes from her, back-handed her again, and reared up over her to unbuckle his belt and pull down his ragged trousers.

'There,' he roared, 'how ya like this?'

Suddenly, Liver-eating Johnson, Jnr., threw his arms back, his mouth open in a retch of agony, as a bullet passed clean through his back and chest, splattering her with blood. The giant of a man tottered to one side, reaching for his daddy's old Colt in his belt holster. He pulled it out, raised it to fire, emptying it, with a howl of anger, at a man who was climbing down the cliffside. The carbine in the young man's hands barked lead again, and Johnson took a step back to go screaming, tumbling and spinning to his death on the rocks below.

Jane could hardly believe it. She looked up into Buck Bradley's grey, concerned eyes as he knelt beside her. 'Are you OK, honey?' He held her in his arms, tight against his rough shirt, patting her back, smoothing her hair from her eyes. 'It's all right now, Jane. It's over. He's gone. Jeez, I guess I got here in the nick of time.' He gently kissed her lips, her cheeks, her eyes. 'Don't worry, that ogre's got his just deserts. He won't bother you no more.'

Eight

At first, just for seconds, Jane Merriman had been tempted to succumb to Buck Bradley's embrace, the warm strength of his arms holding her, his kisses fluttering over her face. It was so good to feel safe, to be consoled, to feel soothed. But she gently eased herself from him, modestly caught her torn dress together to cover her breasts.

'I'm sorry. My face, my lips hurt. They're already beginning to swell up. I'm all bruised from falling down the slope. Buck, we've got to go. Dad's gut-shot bad. We've got to get back to the ranch.'

'Steady, honey,' he said, as she tried to get to her feet. 'You're all shook up. Reno's gone on to the ranch. He'll know what to do.'

'But he was bleeding bad. Oh, God, I hope he's OK. And Sally, he hurt her awful, too, smashed her in the jaw with his gun. The others are all dead.'

She was trembling, uncontrollably, but pushed him away when he tried to hold her close again. 'Come on, we've got to get back.'

He helped her back up the slope and onto the back of the big plodding horse that Johnson had ridden. And set off at a lope on his quarter horse,

Red. They rode at a steady pace until they reached the main trail and she called out, 'Where did you spring from? How did you know?'

'Well,' he drawled, 'the family at the saw mill told me that hulking great brute had come this way the night before so I guessed who he was. As we rode up the trail we met the herd of escaped mustangs. We rounded 'em up and sent 'em skittering back to the ranch. Then I spotted the big fresh hoofprints going along this offshoot trail so I thought I better follow. Lucky I did. Looks like I arrived and saved you from a fate even worse than death.'

'You certainly did.'

'Hey, ain't you noticed something? The hoss I'm riding?'

Jane glanced across. 'Red? Is that Red?'

'It sure is.'

'You've got him back! And Snow Storm? Is he—?'

'Safe an' sound. He'll be waitin' for you.'

Jane was lost for words. It seemed impossible. This man had done so much for her, for them all. Maybe she had misjudged him. 'At least,' she said, 'some good has come out of all this.'

'Yeah, maybe we can still win the championships.'

'Oh,' she sighed, shaking her head as she straddled the big cart horse, pounding along as fast as she could go. 'That's all over for me now.'

'Aw, c'mon.' He couldn't help sneaking a lustful look at the girl's sunburned legs, at her bare breasts jiggling out of the torn dress as she rode, and grinned. 'Where's your ole warrior spirit?' Indeed, with her long hair streaming out behind her she looked like some Amazon princess.

'Look, they've killed my friends. For all I know my father may be dead,' she shouted. 'They've stolen the horses. They've poisoned our dogs. What more do you want of me? I've had enough, Buck. I guess I owe you my life and I'm grateful. But it's all over.'

'Thass OK,' he grinned. 'You don't owe me nuthin'. But one thang's fer sure, they ain't gittin' me down. What I'd like to know is who's behind all this? Who paid Snake Stevens? Who put Ebenezer Johnson up to it, put him on his way? That lunatic was too dumb to work out where you lived by hisself. Who's the puppet-master? I got my suspicions. But the difficulty is proving it.'

'Who do you suspect?'

'Who do you think? Sure, it's fair enough tryin' to nobble *me*, but who would want to put a gal like you out of the contest?'

'Robert Rudge?'

'You got it.'

'So, what are you going to do?'

'I dunno. But I'm working on it.'

When they got to the ranch they found that Reno had bandaged a poultice to Clint Merriman's wound and had got him lying down under blankets, resting. 'He's lost a lot of blood but he should pull through. It's Sally I'm worried about. Her jaw's broke. She's in a lot of pain and I ain't sure what to do.'

Sally was, indeed, in a sorry state, hardly able to see through her swollen eyes, her jaw bleeding and twisted loose. She gasped with pain when she tried to smile on seeing Jane safe. In strangulated tones she tried to say to Reno, 'I'm gonna be as ugly a sonuvagun as you.'

'You'll never be *that* ugly, Sally,' Reno replied. 'You'll allus be as sweet as a bowl of honey to me.'

'There's a doctor at Big Cedar,' Jane said. 'Somebody had better go fetch him. She needs proper attention.'

'I'm on my way,' Reno went to leap on his piebald.

'It looks like we got a lot of buryin' to do,' Buck said, as he and Jane sat alone in the kitchen. 'I blame myself for not getting back quicker. I shouldn't have hung around that rodeo at Fort Worth. If we'd got back last night we mighta stopped all this.'

'There's no need to blame yourself.' Jane poured him a mug of coffee from the pot. 'You've done all you could do.'

The autumn leaves had begun to blow away. The buryings had been done and headboards raised over them. The ranch buildings had been tidied up. There was much to do with three hands lost, but Buck Bradley was beginning to feel restless. It would soon be the big championships at Oklahoma City. First he needed to pick up points at a number of smaller rodeos if he was going to have any chance of beating Dusty Roberts.

'Why so gloomy?' Jane was putting Snow Storm through his paces; she rode past him as he leaned over the corral rail. 'You've got the look of a hobbled mustang.'

'Aw, nuthin',' he muttered, chewing at a straw. 'Just thinkin' how well you two could do in the champeen-ships.'

'Look.' She rode across to him. 'Why don't you go? It's obvious rodeo's all you live for. But me, I've got to stay. There's the stock to look after and I'm going into horse-doctoring from now on. Rodeo doesn't interest me.'

'It's you I'm worried about, Jane. I don't want to leave you here. You and the horse would be safer with me. What we ought to do is hide him out some place until the championships and then surprise 'em all.'

'Don't be silly. Who would run this place, look after Dad?'

'I think your father would be the first to tell you to go. He's a rodeo man, too. Winning the championships is all he's ever dreamed of. You'd be doing it for him. Sally's on her feet; she could look after him. You could soon get a couple more ranch-hands. 'Come on, Jane, come with me. You know you want to.'

'I don't know any such thing. It ain't as easy as you think, Buck, to run this place. But you and Reno go. We'll be OK.'

Jane had had a hard struggle to care for her invalids and keep the horse ranch going on her own. Black Hawk's widow had gone into a pining trance since his death and went about her chores like a zombie. Jane had to help her with the housework, the cooking, washing, bedmaking, milking, wood chopping, and sweeping, as well as go back and forth lugging buckets of water and caring for the horses and stock, feeding the chickens, collecting eggs, doing the hundred-and-one things that needed doing around a ranch. Fortunately, her father was much improved after two weeks and back on his crutches, or in his wheelchair, and Sally, still on liquids, with her jaw wired- up, was feeling more like her old self and able to help.

But Jane had found it hard to recruit men to replace the three who had been killed. For a start there were not many available in this vast forest area. Those that were had their own farms to run or were engaged by the big lumber firm that had been given the contract to work the Indians' land. However, she had been able to get a tall, gangling, ex-rodeo rider, Lance, who had been badly kicked by a bull and wasn't quite right in the head. He rarely spoke and had the understanding of a child, but he was able to do simple tasks like cleaning tack, or scything hay.

In the morning, Buck was still there. 'Maybe,' he muttered to Reno, 'I oughta try to romance her into comin' along.'

'You can try, boy, but I don't go much on your chances.'

Jane, after seeing to the invalids, was tending to Snow Storm, mixing linseed oil in his bran to make his coat shine. Then she was tempting him with a carrot holding it to one side then the other so it would exercise his neck tendons. On the spur of the moment she tried a trick she had learned as a girl, putting the carrot in her teeth and letting the stallion munch down it until they were almost nose to nose. She let the horse chomp it, after which he held his head high, flickering his lips at her to give her a 'kiss'.

'Hey, I sure see who my competition is.' Buck Bradley had stepped up quietly behind her and was smoothing her well-formed *derriére* with his hands. 'Is he the only one who gets a kiss?'

Jane froze, a chill going down her spine at the

nearness of his presence, and his touch. 'Please don't do that. Don't you realize how insulting it is to a girl?'

'It ain't intended as an insult, Jane,' he murmured. 'I just find it hard to keep my hands off your body.'

'Just leave me be, Buck.' She half-turned to face him. 'I thought I'd made it clear. I'm one gal you're not going to be rolling in the hay.'

'You sure about that? You sure you don't want me to?'

'Yes, I'm sure. And even if I'm not, I'm not going to, because how long would it last?'

'Who knows,' he said, trying to sweeten her. 'You never can tell.'

'Yeah, well, I know. I know that if I did, pretty soon, one of these days, you'd be riding away over those hills without looking back.'

'Aw, come on, Jane,' he drawled, touching her waist. 'Loosen up.'

But he quickly retreated as the stallion made a move for him, butting him with his head, whinnying shrilly, raising his fore-hoofs in a stomping dance of anger.'

'Hell!' Buck leapt for safety, backing out of the stable door.

'Go on, get him, Storm.' Jane Merriman shrilled with laughter. 'I've never seen a cowboy move so fast.'

'Yeah,' Buck agreed, from safety. 'I've seen what a stallion like that can do. I'll be needing my *cojones* for a while. I got big plans for 'em.'

'Yes, well don't include me. You won't be waltzing me into the woodshed.' She soothed the horse, calming him. 'All right, Snow Storm. You see what you've done, Mr Bradley? You've made him jealous. I think you'd better be on your way.'

'Yeah, well, I will be.' He shrugged. 'You stay with your damn hoss if you prefer him to me.' He strolled over to Red Desert and slung his saddle over his back. 'Me and Reno's got some important dates. There's a rodeo at Antlers. After that it's up to Tishomingo for the Chickasaw festival. Then we're headin' to the south side of Oklahoma City for the Norman fun and games. After that, we'll be ready for the big one.'

Jane watched the lean cowboy, with a tinge of regret, as he tightened his cinch and tied his bedroll secure, swinging up onto the big quarter horse, tugging his hat down over his brow and calling out to Reno, 'You comin', pardner? We got a long ride.'

Buck flicked his fingers to her, waved to Merriman and Sally on the veranda, and straight-backed in the saddle, headed towards the ranch gate. Reno cantered Magic after him.

Jane watched the two men go, hanging onto Snow Storm's head. 'Good luck,' she called, but her words were whipped away in the wind.

Snake Stevens was sitting in an eating-house in Broken Bow when he saw Buck Bradley in his tattered chaps and battered Stetson, ride by on the quarter horse, accompanied by his Indian pal on the patch horse. His fingers automatically snaked towards the Remington revolver in the holster strung to his thigh. His instinct was to rush outside and backshoot both of them and have it over with. But wasn't he in enough trouble? Hadn't he been lucky to escape the hue and cry after him in Texas? Down there they hung up horse-thieves without trial. It was a crime regarded as more heinous than murder in some places. He felt safer back here in the Nations, the natural haunt of fugitives, for there were only a few Indian police to bother about, or the occasional nosy US deputy marshal dispatched from Fort Smith in far-off Arkansas. Most of them didn't live long enough to cause anyone much trouble.

Snake stifled the urge to take revenge on the two rodeo riders. He had just been reading a roughly printed news-sheet, *The Broken Bow Advertiser*. Its banner headline screamed: 'SLAUGHTER AT LAZY RIVER – THREE MEN KILLED – EBENEZER JOHNSON'S FRENZIED BLOODLUST – BRONCO-BUSTER SAVES RANCHER'S DAUGHTER.' So that giant haystack had made a hash of it and Buck Bradley had been playing the hero? It seemed the cowboy could take care of himself. Stevens decided he might need to use more stealth.

It looked like Bradley and Reno were headed for the railroad depot. 'I'll catch up with them two later,' Snake muttered, as he resumed his meal. 'Damn Rudge! He's making me earn my pay.'

Maybe, he thought, this was his chance to go settle with the girl and her stallion. Her crippled father fighting for his life. The ranch hands decimated. She would be on her own.

Nine

Antler's annual rodeo was in full swing, the town in carnival mood, bunting and banners fluttering in the breeze, folks flocked in from far and wide, settlers and Choctaws, with circus people from Hugo adding to the spectacle and colour. The town band was leading the parade of riders down the main street.

Buck Bradley on Red Desert raised his Stetson and acknowledged the cheering crowds lining the route to the arena. 'Hey,' he called to Reno, 'anywhere we can git a stiffener 'fore the bronc-bustin'?'

Reno winked and touched his nose with a forefinger. 'Us redskins can smell booze twenty miles away.' He kneed Magic out of the parade and headed for a cluster of wagons and tents. Liquor had long been officially banned in the Nations, but the Choctaws made their own beer, and now that white settlers were in the majority the law was largely ignored. Many had their own stills out in the woods and whiskey-smuggling was rife.

'Howdy, boys,' Buck yelled, jumping down from Red to join a mob of men sampling moonshine from a barrel on the back of a covered wagon. 'Make way for a man with a thirst.'

'Yay-hey!' A young rider called Curly Wayne sounded like he'd already imbibed a good swig of the fire-water. 'If it ain't ole Buck Bradley. You tryin' to make up points on Dusty? You two both better watch out 'cause I'm catchin' up fast.'

It was true, the curly-headed youngster was the new up and coming rodeo star, hungry for a place in the Cowboy Hall of Fame, as they called it, and not far behind in the placings.

'You better take it easy on that stuff if you're in the bronc-bustin' boy. You need a reasonably clear head,' Buck said. 'Take my advice. I'm just having one snort and a chaser of Choc beer.'

'Listen to the old-timer,' Curly grinned. 'He's worried I cain't take my liquor.'

'Is Dusty here?' Reno asked. 'I ain't seen him.'

'Sure, he's restin' up in his hotel room. Thinks himself too good to mix with us. He don't drink, he hardly eats, he barely weighs eight stone. He don't chase the gals.' Curly gave a hoot, punching the air. 'What the hell's he do with his cash?'

'He's a professional.' Buck took a bite of the evil brew. 'Whoo! This stuff's got the kick of a mule. Maybe he's got the right idea.'

The Westerners stood around talking rodeo shop until a loudhailer announced that the main event of the afternoon, the bronco-busting, would soon commence. Buck, Reno and Curly wandered across to join in the draw for the fiery mustangs each would have to try to ride. Dusty Roberts, with his handler, was already there, and, meeting Buck's eyes, merely gave him a curt nod. He was a lean and mean little riding machine. But he was not invincible. Nobody was in this game.

'Bad luck, Curly,' Buck drawled. 'You've drawn Satan. He spins to the left. He can be dangerous. If he heads for the rails you jump off his back quick.'

'Aw, you're just tryin' to score me outa points,' Curly drawled. 'Danger's what I'm here for. It's the excitement I love. I wanna be like you, Bradley, mad, bad, and dangerous to know.'

'Yeah, well don't overdo it, son.'

The tension and excitement was notably imparted to the crowd as one by one the riders mounted their mustangs and came flying out of the chute. Dusty rode third and put in his customary polished performance as he mastered his plunging, leaping steed, before skipping off to take top marks.

'That li'l guy's got glue in his pants,' Buck muttered. He had drawn to ride sixth and last.

He recalled Jane Merriman arguing with him, saying that she didn't like bronco-riding, claiming it was cruel to the animal. He had heatedly replied, 'There ain't nuthin' cruel about it. Those horses are given the best of care and food. They ain't never had their spirit broke. They enjoy tossing us offen their backs. At least they don't have to go round doin' all those repetitive exercises women put them through. They don't have to earn their living as a farm tool out on the range to be discarded when they're done. A rodeo bronc's a highly-prized piece of horseflesh. Yeah, I'd say when he's out there bucking and kicking his heels he's really having fun, wouldn't you, Reno?'

Jane had accused him of being naïve. Naïve? What the devil was she talking about? 'Wimmin,' he growled. 'I'll never understand 'em.'

Curly was next up, a big cheer greeting the rodeo rider's name. Buck slapped his back. 'Thass the way. Ride him, cowboy!'

Curly lowered himself over the snorting Satan, carefully took his reins. He grinned down at Buck. 'You betcha. You're gonna be eating my dust.'

They were the last words anyone heard him say. He hung onto the spinning, eye-glinting Satan, for a count of six, for too long as the mustang tried to shake this man from his back and headed, noticeably, towards the rails.

'Jump,' Buck gritted out. 'Fer Chris'sakes.'

Too late. Curly tumbled from the bronco's back on the wrong side and there was an audible crack as his head hit the post. Women screamed as Curly lay inert and Satan went bucking and bouncing away. Men ran over to the fallen rider. There was nothing they could do. Curly Wayne was dead, his cranium cracked like an eggshell, his vivid red blood pooling in the dust.

'Aw, hell,' Buck groaned, as he listened to the announcement that in view of the tragic accident the bronco-busting event would be brought to a close. 'They coulda given me my go.'

'Show some respect, Bradley,' one of the judges said, overhearing him. 'A young man's just lost his life. A promising young rider, too. Don't you have any feelings for your own?'

'Aw, yeah, I'm cut up 'bout Curly as much as anyone,' Buck sighed, as he watched the rider being stretchered away. 'But I needed those points.'

'I need a shot,' Reno said. 'You comin'?'

They joined a group of other rodeo riders by the whiskey wagon. Some men sat on barrels in silence and stared at the dust, others conversed in low voices. The death of the popular youngster had put a damper on them all 'Well you cain't say I didn't warn him about that bronc,' Buck gritted out. 'Durned young fool.'

'You staying for the funeral?' Reno asked, refilling their tumblers from the vendor's barrel. It would mean a delay of a few days while Curly's kith and kin gathered.

'Yes,' Buck nodded, deep in thought. 'Of course.'

Jane was concentrating her energies on schooling the sorrel gelding. He had a good shoulder move-ment; he was stepping out well as, on a light lunge rein, he went cantering around the corral. When Panama, as he was known, had first arrived, yes, he had been dangerous. He would get the bit between his teeth, run off, try to leap fences, or turn, at the last moment, and crash into them. To try to stop him the farmer had been putting fiercer and fiercer bits on him. This had only made him more dangerous to ride, and for Jane Merriman, too, when she first tried him.

'He's not a bad horse,' she called out to her father. 'He's frightened, that's all. When he gets out of control the more he's punished, and so the worse he gets. It's a vicious spiral.'

For two weeks now Jane had been gently getting the trust of the sorrel, starting him from scratch with-out a stitch on his head or back, coaxing him to her, so that gradually he wanted to be with her, he wanted to be taught. First she had ridden him with a light hackamore, then progressed to the curb, the simplest and most humane bit, with a low port connected to leather reins, instead of the cruel Spanish chains and spade bits that had damaged his mouth.

Today Jane gently eased the curb bit and bridle onto him and he accepted it with the merest shake of his head, as he did when his saddle was cinched tight. Around the ranch Jane wore a faded pair of Levi Strauss jeans and rode astride for there was nobody to offend: the two Choctaw boys who had been put on the payroll didn't mind, nor Lance, nor her father for that matter, although in public a female was still required to ride side-saddle as a matter of 'decency'.

'You've done wonders with that horse,' her father called to her, softly, so as not to upset her or Panama's concentration. 'I didn't think you had a hope in hell when he first arrived.'

'Oh, he's a good boy,' Jane coaxed him, rubbing between his eyes and gently put a moccasined foot into the stirrup before swinging lightly aboard. 'Now then, boy, ride on.' A nudge from her knee was all it took to send him loping forwards around the corral at a steady pace. She tried to put as little pressure on his mouth as she could and, when she wanted him to stop she just murmured, 'Whoa,' and pressed her weight down into the back of the saddle. Panama came to a steady halt as if the idea had been his own. Horse and rider were one.

'OK, Dad,' Jane smiled. 'It's time to open the gate and try him out on the trail. Can you?'

'Sure.' Clint Merriman hopped along on his crutches and swung the gate wide. 'You better not go in the paddock with Snow Storm. I figure he's been gettin' awful jealous watching you two these past weeks.'

'Yes, I've been neglecting him. I'll give him a good curry-combing and a gallop when I get back.'

'Take care.' Merriman watched her ride Panama out of the Lazy River ranch gate as the indignant Snow Storm pranced along on the other side of the fence, whinnying at them as if to say, 'Hey, it's my turn.'

'Good golly!' Sally came out of the wash-house wiping her hands on her pinafore. 'Is Jane on that horse? That's amazin'.'

'Yeah, she musta inherited my hoss sense. Or Black Hawk's. He always told her not to look a horse in the eye, but to turn half away, coax it to you. The Indians got strange ways with hosses.'

Sally nodded as he limped painfully across on his crutches to sink back on his wicker bed on the veranda. 'It's a durn pity she's given up the shows. She coulda bin a winner.'

'She's adamant, I'm afraid. To tell you the truth, Sally, I'm worried about her. All she does is work. She won't relax. I don't know why she's so set against Buck.'

Sally tried not to grin because it hurt. 'She's sho developed a brick wall 'ginst rodeo riders.'

'Never mind. How about we rustle up a nice cool flask of lemonade, you and I?'

'Yo' mean yo' want me to do the rustlin'? Sure enough, but I'm gonna help yo' drink it.'

110

*

Snake Stevens, still in his disguise of thick beard, tall-crowned Stetson and duster coat was riding along the trail towards the Lazy River ranch when he saw a rider approaching at a fast clip. He moved his mustang into the woods and paused, watching. At first he thought it was a youth in shirt and blue jeans, for Jane had her hair tucked up under her sombrero. But then he detected the movement of her breasts beneath her blouse. 'Hey, now,' he murmured, 'just the gal I'm lookin' for.'

About a hundred yards before she reached him, however, the girl slowed her sorrel, carefully turned him around, and set off back at a spirited canter towards the ranch. Snake let her go. 'No, she ain't seen me,' he muttered. 'Must be just exercisin' the dang hoss. I'm gonna have to wait 'til dark.'

He hung about in the woods, built a small fire and boiled up coffee. The dark, towering pines, so sinister and silent, made him nervous. He needed to get this done and get out of there. His preferred habitat was a crowded saloon, bawdy house or billiards parlour.

When the moon began its climb and night-prowling animals began emitting their shrill calls he went forward, heading through the ranch gates and up through the fenced-off pastures. 'Hey, there's that durn stallion,' he said, catching sight of the spotted Appaloosa grazing in the moonlight. 'Waal, whadda ya know?'

He looked up the hill at the turreted white house, lamps burning in the windows. 'Why bother with the gal? Nobody's gonna brand *me* a woman-killer. This is all I need to do and my job's done.'

He climbed from his mustang, hitched it to a rail, and gave a whistle, drawing his revolver, calling the stallion over, 'Here y'are, Snow Storm, look what I gotcha.' He held out his free hand, climbing over the rail, and the inquisitive beast came cantering over, his hoofs stomping on the turf. His eyes bulged and his nostrils quivered as he scented the man, and suddenly he backed away as if sensing something wrong. But Stevens snatched hold of his hackamore around his ears and jaw. He pulled the stallion to him as the Appaloosa struggled, raising the revolver to his temple, and fired. The stallion collapsed, his knees buckling, frothing blood.

Snake put another bullet into his brain and watched him die.

'Right,' he said, backing away, looking-up at the house, vaulting the rail, and swinging back on his mustang. 'Let's git outa here.'

Outside Antlers, at the town graveyard, a few days later, a guard of honour of rodeo riders took Curly Wayne's coffin from the horse-drawn hearse and bore him slowly on their shoulders towards the newly-dug grave.

Curly's mother, in black, gave a wailing sob as she watched the coffin being lowered into the dark hole. Her husband caught hold of her to prevent her falling. Other friends and family stood around in a mournful circle.

'He's gone to the Green Valley,' the preacher intoned. 'He's gone to fresh pastures where he can roam free. He's gone to a better land than this world of treachery and turmoil that you and I know. Curly rode the knocks and blows that life can hand out in an honest and cheerful way. But he was cut down in his prime by one kick too many and we send his soul to you, Father, with our prayers that you open the gate to the Green Pasture for him.'

Buck Bradley nudged Reno and droned, 'Ashes to ashes, dust to dust, if the liquor don't git ye, the wimmin must. Don't this holy Joe go on?'

The preacher was a plump, pink man in a black suit and spectacles, who had greeted Buck to the burying with a limp, damp handshake – not a hand that had ever done any hard digging. He left that to the two Indian helpers in the graveyard of his mission house, who stood there now, spades in hands, waiting to shovel earth back in on the coffin.

'Friends,' the preacher called to the good crowd who had gathered for the funeral, 'as the coffin is lowered we will conclude with that fine old hymn, "We'll be with you by and by". Number 136 in your hymn books.'

As the mournful singing began, and Curly's coffin was lowered on ropes, men stepped forward to take a handful of earth, toss it on the pine box and mutter their own last words.

A wall of stones surrounded the churchyard and on the trail out of town alongside it, Snake Stevens was sitting a horse rented from the livery for a day. He carefully watched the group of mourners and levered a bullet into his carbine, raising it to his shoulder. 'Yeah, you can say your prayers, Bradley.'

He had decided that as he had come all this way to

find the rodeo rider he had better deal with him before he left town. He had checked that a locomotive would be leaving Antlers just after the scheduled time of the funeral and heading north and he planned to be on it. But, first, Bradley. As the hymn-singing drifted to him, he saw that the wrangler, in his stetson and chaps, was standing alongside the preacher, holding a hymn book in one hand. He was no more than seventy paces away. He couldn't miss.

'Now!' Snake hissed, but the instant he squeezed the trigger Bradley knelt to pick up a fistful of dirt to toss on the box. The plump little preacher, instead, squawked and toppled into the grave. 'Shee-it!'

As a bullet whanged past his hat and a shot cracked out, Buck, still kneeling saw the preacher land on the coffin, his hymn book still clutched in his hands, but a red hole in his temple from which blood leaked. He stared down for a few seconds and coming to his senses, yelled, 'Hit the dust, fer Chris'sakes, everybody. We're bein' shot at.'

Pa-dang! Another bullet whined and ricocheted off a gravestone as men and women yelled, screamed and scattered. Pa-chong! That one nearly sliced off Buck's ear as he peered up to see where the shooting was coming from. He raised his own Smith & Wesson and snapped out three shots at the bearded horseman in a flapping duster coat out on the road. Who the hell was he? Another maniac?

'What's he wanna kill the preacher for?' he yelled at Reno.

'It ain't the preacher he wants dead,' Reno gritted out, bringing his own carbine into play. 'It's you.'

'Me? What 'n hell fer? What I done to him? I ain't

never seen the *hombre* before.'

'Well, he ain't waitin' to let us know.'

Indeed, cursing his bad luck, Snake Stevens, suddenly under close fire, had jerked his mustang's head around, spurred him, viciously, and set off back along the dusty trail into town.

'C'mon, less git after him.'

Bradley spun his revolver back into his holster, ran and took a vaulting leap onto the back of Red Desert, as other men blazed guns at the back of the escaping assassin. 'Make way, men, hold your fire. I'm going after him.'

Red Desert didn't need any spurring or whipping, he was always ready for a race. One shout from Buck and he was pounding away along the white, curving trail back towards Antlers, with Reno on Magic doing their best to stay with them.

Whoo-whoooh! The long drawn-out wail of the 'Katie's' steam siren greeted them and they saw the little locomotive shunting out a column of smoke from its stack as it went rattling out of Antlers, its rods pummelling back and forth rhythmically, driving its big wheels, pulling two carriages, a box car, and caboose. It had already achieved top speed of thirty miles an hour when the rider with his duster coat flapping veered his horse off the trail and across the prairie towards it.

Buck was gaining on him, pulling his .44 to fire wildly at his back as he raced along. But the gunman was a good seventy paces in front of him and going in a semi-circle to gallop alongside the Puffing Billy. He looked back desperately, rattled along the side of the single track, then leapt from the saddle to clutch at the rail of the viewing platform before swinging himself onto the caboose, as his abandoned mustang dropped back and away from him.

Snake Stevens had abandoned the carbine in the mustang's boot, too, but he drew his silver-engraved Remington revolver, and, giving a maniacal laugh, let the pursuing rodeo rider have his lead. 'Take that, you lousy range rat. Die, damn you! Die!'

Buck ducked as the bullets buzzed about him like fierce bees on the attack, and whirled Red Desert to a halt. There was no way he could catch up and take him, except suicidally.

Defiantly, he fired the last bullet in his .44 at the man in the duster, who stood grinning, gun blazing, on the viewing platform as the train jogged on its way. Soon it was just a dot in the distance and a drifting cloud of steam and smoke.

'Who the hell was he?'

'Beats me,' Reno gasped, as he caught up. 'Maybe another of Rudge's hitmen. You better watch your back, boy.'

'Yep, another move in the dirty tricks game. These guys sure don't want me at the championships. Is the preacher dead?'

'Waal, he sure ain't alive.'

'That's the last funeral I'm gonna attend.'

'Yeah, unless, maybe, it's your own.'

Jane stood beside the huge grave she and the two Choctaw youths had dug and used horses and ropes to drag the corpse of the Appaloosa stallion into it. She wiped a drip of sweat from her nose as she shovelled dirt over him. She couldn't bear to think of him being pecked at by the buzzards. She took a rest and stared at her father in his wheelchair. 'Dad, they can't do this to us. I've had enough.'

Merriman considered her: she looked on the point of collapse. 'Don't take it too hard, Jane. It's only a horse.'

'Only a horse?' she snapped. 'Waltzing Boy trusted us. He never hurt anybody.'

'Well, it looks like whoever did it made a mistake. They must have thought he was Snow Storm.'

Jane shovelled more dirt on and sighed. 'What's the difference?'

'The difference is we've still got Snow Storm.'

'Yes, we have.' Jane tossed the shovel away and stood erect. 'And, you know what, I'm not going to let these people, these monsters, walk all over us.'

'Think about this, Jane. Don't do anything foolish.'

'I have thought about it. I was going to wash my hands of them, try to forget it all, live like a nun the rest of my life. But this, this is too much. I'm going to Oklahoma City, Dad. I'm going to compete.'

Merriman considered this for a minute, then nodded and smiled. 'Let me tell you something, Jane: You're one of the finest horsemasters I've ever seen, and I'm not just saying that. I've seen a few. You've a God-given talent, Daughter. Your timing, your movement, they're impeccable. You can win at Oklahoma City. I only wish I could come with you.'

'I wish you could, Dad, but I'll be OK on my own. I'm going to go up to the house and get myself and Snow Storm ready.' She forced a smile. 'They say its a sin not to capitalize on what God gave you. I'll go look for Buck and Reno.'

'Yeah, and don't forget you're a mighty fine-looking young woman when you *do* meet Buck Bradley. We could do with a man and some gran'kids around this place.'

Jane flashed him another smile. 'That's not exactly part of the deal.'

'No? Still, don't forget I've got money riding on you. I thought I'd get in fast while the odds were good.'

Ten

'You wanna make a change, Buck?' Reno asked, as he sat Magic, and looked across at Bradley. 'You do the hazin' and I'll jump the durn bull.'

He could see that the usually cocksure Bradley was not his customary self, constantly exercising the wrist that had been giving him trouble. In fact, he looked decidedly worried as he pulled on his leather gloves ready for their turn in the bull-dogging event at Tishomingo festival and rodeo.

'What's the point of that?' Buck gathered the reins of Red Desert. 'I'm here to win the points, not for you to.'

'Yeah, but you'll be gettin' nothin' if that wrist gives out. And you'll be outa the contests for good. You gotta rest it, Buck.'

'You do your job.' Bradley scowled across from his left-hand side of the chute. 'I'll do mine.'

There was a big crowd around the arena and a lot of money changing hands on Bradley winning this. Unluckily, they didn't know about the sprain to his wrist.

'Right, you ready?' Buck asked.

Reno was the hazer, and, as such, stationed on the

right-hand side of the chute. As soon as the fully grown bullock was released it was his job to chase after it and haze it, yelling, and slapping his lariat, to keep it going in a straight line.

Buck's job was to chase after it on its left-hand side, leap from the saddle and haul it to the ground. The throwing of an 800-pound bullock at full pelt is not as easy as it sounds. The beasts don't suffer, apart from their dignity. It's the cowboys who often get hurt.

As their names were announced through the loud-hailer, a cheer went up. Buck had proved to be the favourite in this event. Today he bit his lower lip nervously as he eased his fingers in the gloves and sat poised on his horse ready for the chase.

Red Desert knew what to do; he only needed a prick of the spurs. The bell clanged, the chute swung open and the bullock charged out, with Reno racing alongside it to keep it in line. Red was after it like a whippet after a hare. He really seemed to enjoy this sport. And it also seemed like he knew they had to do well if they were to stay in the finals – maybe he just sensed Buck's tension?

They were pounding alongside. Buck hurled himself from the saddle, landed on top of the fleeing beast, wrapped an arm around the animal's horns, took his nose in the crook of his elbow, dug his heels into the dust, gave an almighty twist to the bullock's neck and flipped him, first time, tumbling over onto his side. When his flanks hit the dust the bell clanged again. The judge was checking his stopwatch. The numerals were put up on the board – 4. 4 seconds.

The crowd exploded, yelling, tossing hats in the

air. It was a great score. One of the greatest they had ever seen. Buck got to his feet, grinned as the bullock got up and tottered away. Then he threw his own hat spinning into the air in a spirit of wild delirium. Let Dusty Roberts do better than that!

He hadn't needed to put much pressure on his wrist. It was his shoulders, forearms and biceps that took the strain, plus perfect timing in the first place. He retrieved his battered Stetson, leaped onto Red Desert and did a canter around the arena acknowledging the applause.

'See, what did I tell you,' he called to Reno. 'If we do as well in the steer-roping we'll be on level-pegging with Roberts.'

'He's up next.' They had taken their horses out of the arena. 'Come on, or we'll miss it.'

'Hey, pard,' Buck called to one of the kids who hung around hero-worshipping the rodeo stars. 'Wanna earn a quarter? Hang onto Red Desert. I gotta see this.'

The boy grinned his delight. 'Sure thing, Buck.'

Bradley and Reno climbed up onto the corral fence as Roberts went ripping out after his bullock. But his hazer hadn't quite caught the critter and, as Dusty prepared his leap, the bullock swung away to the right in front of the hazer's hoofs. It was too late. Roberts hit the dust without touching him. He sat up on his backside, spitting hoss-shit, and had a tantrum, pummelling the ground amid the laughter and catcalls. Buck and Reno yelled and slapped gloved hands. The great Dusty Roberts was losing points fast.

'Waal, if it ain't the gal from the Lazy River ranch.'

Buck's smile widened as he met the eyes of Jane Merriman. 'What in hell are you doin' here?'

'You may not believe it' – she returned his smile – 'but looking for you.'

'You don't say?' Might I ask why?'

'Yes, I'm looking for protection.' She filled him in on what had happened to Waltzing Boy. 'You are my best bet.'

Buck and Reno had been celebrating their victories at Toshomingo and, with whiskey inside them, were in a wild mood as, behind them, Chickasaw warriors, in feathers and paint, were dancing like strange exotic birds to the chanting of their elders and women and the banging of war drums.

But the sight of Jane and her bad news about Waltzing Boy sobered them. 'Who would do a thing like that, the lousy snake in the grass.'

'Snake?'

'You mean Stevens?'

'No, even he wouldn't be so low, would he?'

'If he's struck once,' Buck said, 'when he's realized his mistake he'll strike again. Where you got Snow Storm?'

'In the corral, hobbled, behind the livery. They didn't have any free stalls. And I couldn't find a bed for myself. The hotels are full.'

'Yuh. It's rodeo. They're sleepin' twenty to a room.'

'What you need,' Reno said, 'is a glass of beer. How's Sally?'

'Oh, she's doing fine. To tell you the truth, that sounds a good idea. I'm parched. I never thought I'd find you.'

They all imbibed more than one and, in fine spirits, looked around the town at folks having fun, dancing, banjo-plucking, involved in log-cutting contests or climbing the greasy pole. Buck took a turn at horseshoe pitching, and they wandered on their way. He slipped an arm around Jane's slender waist and, for once, she did not resist, but slipped her own fingers into the back pocket of his jeans. It felt good swinging along to his stride.

'You better bring Snow Storm over to where we're camped. Tomorrow we're heading for Norman. It's the last rodeo before the big one. Me and Reno need to make a few more points.'

'Yeah, but Jane's is just a straightforward contest at Oklahoma City,' Reno pointed out. 'She's already got her name entered. Why don't we take Snow Storm over to Elk City? I got friends of my people there. We can hide him 'til the big day.'

'That's not a bad idea, old son,' Buck said.

It had grown dark by now, so they collected Snow Storm and led him out to their camp on the edge of town. 'Who wants to be in a hotel room?' Buck shouted out. 'There ain't nuthin' like sleepin' out under the stars.'

'Well, I don't mind,' Jane said. 'I got my bedroll.'

When Reno had turned in, Buck and Jane sat, leaning back on their saddles, staring into the glowing embers of the fire. 'You heard what happened to Curly?'

'Yes, I did. You know now why I don't want to get mixed up with a rodeo rider. I don't want to spend my life waiting to see him being stomped to death.'

'That's the risk you take, Jane. Any kind of horse-handling is a dangerous game. But I wouldn't be without it.'

'You don't care you might get your head kicked in to a useless turnip and end up like poor old Lance?'

' 'Course I care. But a man can git drunk and git his head crushed by a wagon wheel. Thass life.'

'It's not my idea of life.'

'So, with you a rodeo rider's out?'

'You're all love 'em and leave 'em kinda guys. You know that. To you life's one long carnival of rodeos and festivals and getting drunk and flittin' like a butterfly among all them pretty young flowers.'

'Yuh?' Buck stood up, caught her hand and pulled her up close to him. 'Sure, there's been some pretty young thangs. Sure, I've sowed my wild oats. But I been careful. Nobody got hurt. They're all a haze to me. There's only one face I think of, Jane, that's yours. You know, gal, I could gaze at you fer the rest of my life.'

'Oh, yeah? How many gals you said that to?' But she could hear the Indian drums pounding away in the background, as they would pound all night long, and could feel her own blood pounding through her, warning her, as she felt his arms, strong and comforting, around her, smelt his masculine smell, felt herself slipping, her defences falling away. His husky voice stroked like a caress and, even though she was aware it was a seduction he might have practiced many times, she could not resist. 'Don't hurt me, Buck. For me it's all or nuthin'. I need a forever kind of man.'

'How do you know I don't feel that way, Jane? I know you been badly damaged like them hosses you

124

treat. But ain't that what you say of them, they gotta learn to trust again?'

'Buck, I guess you win. I'm gonna trust you tonight. I'm gonna hope your love lasts longer than the eight-second count.' It was as if she were melting, as she kissed him, as if all her fears and resolutions were flowing away. Perhaps her need was as wild as his? She just couldn't fight it any more. As of one accord they fell back down to lie on his bed-roll and, as he pulled her into him, she murmured, 'Hell, who wants to be a nun, anyhow?'

'Let's go for the ride, babe. Let's enjoy every second of it.'

Jane could not help laughing as she looked into his mischievous eyes. 'Oh, God, Buck, that's the lamest line I ever heard.' But she twisted her fingers into his thick hair and kissed him harder.

Eleven

Oklahoma City had been until recent years just a camp ground for drovers coming up the Chisholm trail. But since the big land-rush and the spread of the railroads into the Territory, it had developed into a bustling business centre. On wide streets there were stores, banks, hotels, real estate offices, liveries, saloons, corrals and a meat market all servicing the outlying ranching communities.

Most of the buildings were gimcrack wooden false-fronts, but dominating Main Street was The Plainsman Hotel, an impressive Victorian three-storey structure of red brick. Here the wealthy wined and dined. And they demanded the best.

Robert Rudge had booked himself, his wife and daughter, into a suite of rooms, one of which he used as his office. As a leading organizer of the Oklahoma Rodeo Finals he lavished hospitality on visiting bigwigs and took the opportunity to clinch business deals. He was tying his cravat on the morning before the big event when there was a rap on the door and he called to his burly bodyguard, Jake Curtis, 'See who that is.'

Curtis eased the revolver in his belt and opened

the door. For moments he did not recognize the thin, bearded man, with his slicked-back hair, in his torn duster coat. 'It's Snake . . . ain't it?'

Stevens pushed past him. 'Who the hell you think it is?'

'Snake?' Rudge turned from the mirror, buttoning the gold-thread waistcoat over his white linen shirt. 'What are you doing here?'

'What you think? I've come for the rest of my cash.'

'What d'ye mean? It's you should be returning my down payment. You ain't done nothin' yet.'

He, too, was surprised by Snake's appearance. The snappy card-sharp of not long before, now looked dirty, dusty and weatherbeaten: a fugitive. But the cadaverous face, and the snakelike, darting eyes that met his own with cold hostility could belong to no other man. 'What you talkin' about? I've been all the way down to Texas tryin' to get rid of those damn horses. Ace and McCafferty have been killed doin' your dirty work. I was lucky to get out in one piece. Agreed, I haven't nailed Bradley yet, but I'll get him, doncha worry. I've been to a helluva lot of trouble over this. I've been all the way out into the durn wilderness to the Lazy River ranch. The girl won't be competing. Snow Storm's dead.'

'You're crazy. Don't you read the news sheets?' Rudge pulled on the frock coat of his pearl grey suit and picked up a copy of *The Oklahoma City Times*, tossing it to him, pointing to the front story. 'That mountain man failed, and so have you, Snake, all along the line.'

Stevens jaw dropped.

ATTEMPT TO KILL APPALOOSA CHAMPION FOILED.
Fears for the life of Snow Storm, one of the leading contenders in the Ladies Equestrian Final, were resolved when the stallion and his rider, Miss Jane Merriman, arrived in Oklahoma City last night. A bungling attempt to block her entry resulted in Snow Storm's stable companion, Waltzing Boy, being gunned down. Miss Merriman recently survived a murderous attempt on her own life in which three of her ranch hands were slaughtered, and there were strong doubts that she would be competing. But the brave beauty from Lazy River told *The Times*, "I will definitely be riding tomorrow and doing my best to win".

'That ain't possible,' Snake snarled. 'I shot that spotted stallion in the head.'

'You got the wrong Appaloosa, you fool,' Rudge shouted. 'Look what a mess you've got me into now. I'm being implicated in this.'

Snake read some more.

Miss Merriman's main contender is Rowena Rudge, daughter of Oklahoma oilman, Robert Rudge. There have been suggestions that his one-time employee, 'Snake' Stevens, was the horse's hitman. He was on the run after attempting to steal Snow Storm and Red Desert, rodeo rider Buck Bradley's renowned quarter horse. Stevens, wanted for homicide of a railroad guard, is said to be armed and dangerous.

Meanwhile, after some dust-biting bouts throughout the Territory, Bradley is almost neck-to-neck with Dusty Roberts, and, in spite of attempts on his own life, is hellbent on reaping honours at Oklahoma City.

Mr Robert Rudge, himself, denied having any association with the fugitive Stevens. "I totally deplore these dastardly attempts by persons unknown to sway the outcome of our wonderful rodeo. All I can say is, I hope the best contestants win".

Snake's Adam's apple gulped as he laid down the news-sheet. 'Hell,' he snarled, pulling his duster aside, his fingers playing over the butt of his ornate Remington. 'That don't mean I ain't earned the rest of my money. I need it, Rudge. I gotta get outa this territory.'

'You're bad news, Snake.' Rudge eyed the gunman and his revolver apprehensively as he lit a cigar and glanced at Jake Curtis. 'You ain't earned an extra cent. You're finished hereabouts. I want nothin' to do with you. Just get outa here. Go on, scram, 'fore I have you thrown out.'

'Give me my cash, you lousy piece of trash, unless you want what I know about you spread all over that news-sheet.'

Rudge pursed his lips and emitted cigar smoke, considering him. 'You wouldn't do that, Snake. You ain't that much of a snake in the grass, are you? I'm warning you, that would be the last thing you ever did.'

'No?' Stevens glanced around furtively. 'Just give me a thousand and I'll finish this for you. I'll kill Bradley and Snow Storm for you. They shouldn't be hard to find in this city.'

Rudge sighed and shrugged, going to his desk. He produced a wad of greenbacks from the drawer. 'I hope I ain't throwing good money after bad. You've missed out all along the line, Snake. Don't miss out this time.'

Stevens snatched the money and flicked through it. 'I won't miss.'

As he headed for the door Rudge called out, 'Don't ever come near me again, Stevens. It's too dangerous. Look, you concentrate on getting Bradley. Jake, here, will kill that stallion. I can rely on *him*. You got any messages, well, they got one of these newfangled Bell's telephones wired to the hotel here. You use that.'

Jane had brought Snow Storm into the city with a dust cloth over his hide. She had hoped that with all the folks, horses and prize cattle converging on the arena for the three-day event she might go unseen. But she had been noticed and, even though she hid out in a livery stable down by the railroad tracks, a reporter from the *City Times* tracked her down and more-or-less forced her to answer his questions. But the story that broke was not the sort of publicity she wanted.

'You gonna be OK for a coupla hours?' Reno asked. 'I gotta go try to find Buck. We got the bulldoggin' and bull-ropin' events first thing this morning.'

'Sure, I'll be fine.' Jane was polishing Snow Storm's show harness in readiness. 'When you find Buck bring him back here.'

Reno had been gone two hours. Jane lay back in the hay and was so exhausted she drifted off into sleep. She was unaware of the stable door opening and Jake Curtis stepping inside. He did not notice the sleeping girl, his attention drawn primarily to the Appaloosa. The horse was calmly tossing hay about in his stall. Like Ebenezer, Jake had come prepared with a bag of sugar laced with strychnine - enough to kill six horses.

'Here, pal,' he coaxed, 'Come and git it.' The big stallion turned his head to him enquiringly, but continued to tug at his feed in the far corner. 'Come on!' Jake opened the stall gate and stepped inside. 'Look what I got ya.'

'What the hell are you doing?' Jane opened her eyes and saw the huge, shadowy figure of the man. 'Get away from that horse.' Once again in her lifetime she wished she owned a gun, but she jumped to her feet and picked up a pitchfork instead, advancing on him. 'Keep away from that horse. Snow Storm!' She wanted to distract the stallion from whatever the man had in his hand.

'Clear off, you bitch.' Jake turned, put the bait aside, and stepped out of the stall to deal with the girl. When she lunged the vicious prongs at him he dodged aside, caught the fork in one hand, and gave her a crack across the face with his right fist. 'Keep out of this.'

Jane screamed but hung onto the pitchfork, as the big man punched and back-handed her, sending her sprawling. 'No!'

The stallion charged out of his stall, hitting Curtis at full speed with his mouth open, his teeth bared. The man toppled backwards, trying to pull out his Colt as the horse reared, whinnied, squealing his anger, flailing his hooves. It was Curtis's turn to scream, 'No!' Snow Storm was on him, sinking his teeth into his loins, biting clean through his testicles. 'No! Aaaargh. . . .'

Jane stared in horror as the stallion squealed and snorted and stamped on the man beneath him as he screamed.

'No!' she cried out. 'No, Snow Storm. No!'

Ears laid back, the stallion appeared to hear her. He tossed the limp man away, almost contemptuously. He slowly turned and did a high-stepping walk around the stable, his neck arched, his nostrils flared, his tail stuck out, a terrifying and beautiful sight.

'No,' she whispered, as he stood before her, trembling. She climbed, fearfully, to her feet, unsure of his anger, avoiding his eyes, but soothing, stroking his powerful neck and shoulders. 'Good boy. It's all over. 'She led him back into his stall, and hung her arms around his neck. 'Snow Storm, thank you. I love you. I won't let them hurt you. Don't worry, boy. You did right to protect me.'

Jake had ceased retching his panic and agony. He was unconscious. His blood was oozing across the cobbles. Jane was about to run for the doctor. 'I think it will be too late,' she whispered. 'And I think it served him right.'

*

Main Street was packed for the big parade led by contestants in the rodeo on their strutting horses. Buck and Reno rode on either side of Jane, waving to the crowd, but keeping their eyes peeled for trouble.

Dusty Roberts was not going to give in without a fierce fight. The big arena outside town was packed for the opening events, the pony races, the wild horse riding and bull-dogging. It was non-stop action, the cowboys whooping and howling as they chased their targets. Buck and Reno did reasonably well without cheating. Dusty used tricks like biting into his bullock's lip to make it submit to a throw. The judges didn't seem to notice.

The bull-roping was a different kettle of fish. They had drawn a roan steer who came out of the chute like a rocket, a real blue screamer. Reno and Buck had to go after him at full gallop. As Reno hazed him, or tried to, Buck swung his lariat, spinning the noose wide as he hung on to the back of Red Desert. The critter was getting away, jumping like a kangaroo. Buck was forced to make a desperate long throw, which more by luck than judgement dropped over the steer's horns. He slammed Red into a spin and snapped the steer into the dust wondering what had hit him. They clocked a poor time. Dusty was in the lead again.

By noon the rowdy kick-off to the rodeo came to a close with the prize-giving for those events. Dusty went up to take first prize. Rudge was among the officials on the flag-bedecked podium, and his wife, in a

133

straw sunhat smothered with flowers, and a cotton summer dress, had again been given the honour of presenting prize money.

Buck and Reno had only made third. Buck rode up and met Rudge's swarthy sneering regard with his flinty grey eyes. 'How you ever git mixed up with him?' he muttered to Rowena as he moved along to her and she leaned forward to give him his rosette, her low-cut dress revealing her bounteous charms. 'How about meeting me for a siesta at Shelby's Hotel down town?'

Rowena looked momentarily surprised, but her green eyes sparkled with wickedness and she pressed both her cupped hands over his and murmured. 'Three?'

He nodded and winked and raised his hand to the crowd as he cantered out of the arena. The city council had organized their annual exposition, as they called it, on a big scale, with prize money both donated by sponsors and raised by charging admittance fee to the raised seats around the arena. Nearly every seat was taken. After an intermission for lunch, and some fun events like chasing a greased pig, the ladies' equitation events would commence at three o'clock.

Buck made his way past the spielers outside tented sideshows and joined Reno and Jane at a spot they had chosen with grazing for their horses. The girl, in her bespangled show dress, and straw sombrero, began grooming Snow Storm, tying ribbons into his mane, and arranging the white leather crupper along his back and under his tail. The idea of the latter was to encourage him to hold his long tail up.

Extra points were awarded if head and tail were carried well in a spirited walk.

'Ain't you gonna ginger him up?' Reno asked.

'No. That's awful. And illegal.' She well knew that more ruthless competitors might push a piece of ginger into a horse's rectum. 'I wouldn't be so cruel to Snow Storm. Anyway, he's spirited enough as it is.'

She was pleasant enough to Reno, but was cool to Buck. She declined his invitation to go across to the refreshment tent. 'I'm busy,' she replied.

Love? Huh! she thought, as she watched him go. One night of passion at Tishomingo since when they had been kept apart, forced to hide out. In the big parades they waved to the folks but their smiles hid tension as they searched windows and roof-tops for sharp shooters. Any moment a bullet might plough into any one of them. It was no fun. The constant fear of another execution attempt was playing hell with their nerves.

Now, as Jane looked across and saw Buck knocking back whiskey with his rodeo pals and grinning amiably among a flock of fawning farm girls as they begged him to sign their programmes, her suspicions rose. Maybe their one night was just that? She tried to swallow the jealousy that surged up in her but she had seen how Rowena Rudge had squeezed the rodeo rider's hand, smiled and spoken to him. Her woman's intuition told her that something was going on. When Buck Bradley returned her temper snapped.

'I . . . uh . . . I won't be able to watch you ride this afternoon,' he said. 'I got somethang to do.'

'Oh, yes?' Her face appeared to drain of colour as she turned her vivid blue eyes on him. 'You haven't changed, *have* you?'

'What do you mean?' he protested. 'Look, it's only the schooling events this afternoon, ain't it? I'll be there cheering you on tonight in the jumping final.'

'You needn't bother.' She turned back to grooming the horse, freezing him out. '*Only* the schooling, is it? No doubt you've got more pleasant things to do.' She turned her eyes back on him, blazing with anger. 'I saw the way that woman looked at you. I'm not a fool.'

'It ain't what you think, Jane. I just gotta go and see her.' He swung up on to Red Desert and collected the reins. 'Good luck.'

'Ha!' "Good luck, but I've got to go to see her". Is that all you've got to say? Some confidence you give a girl.' She gave a gasp of contempt as she stared at him and stood tall proud and scorned, a chill in her. 'I guess I asked for this. I should have known. Go, then. Go to hell.'

As Buck went to ride away, Reno ran after him and grabbed the reins. 'Why you doin' this to her? Why now?'

'Look, Rudge may be as crooked as a bull's pizzle, but I got a few tricks up my sleeve.'

'You just wanna take cheap revenge on him with his wife.'

'It ain't that. Look after her.' And he sent Red cantering away without looking back.

Robert Rudge was reclining on a sofa in his hotel

suite having lunch of cold chicken. He watched his wife titivating herself before the mirror. 'You're putting a lot of paint and powder on, aincha, to sit out in the sun?'

'I won't be there. I've a fitting with my dressmaker at two-thirty. It will take all afternoon.' She sprayed some perfume around and down her bosom. 'You had better get back to the judging, hadn't you, dear? Tell Rachel I'm sorry I can't be there.'

'She's not going to like it. Why not cancel the fitting?'

'I can't. I'll take the buggy. I might go for a little drive afterwards, get some air.'

'Do what the hell you like.'

When she had gone, he finished the chicken, wiped his greasy palms, and read the newspaper. At ten to three he groaned. 'Guess I better be getting back.' As he was about to leave the telephone rang. 'Yeah?' he grunted into the mouthpiece.

'You oughta watch that wife of yourn,' a voice said.

'What?' he shouted. 'Who is this?'

'A well-wisher. You know where she is?'

'Yes, at the dressmaker's.'

'You oughta try the Shelby Hotel. You might find her in bed with Buck Bradley.'

Rudge stood like a pole-axed bull as the caller rang off. Anger boiled up in him like a poisonous red cloud. He picked up the plate of bones and hurled it at a wall. He paced about the room, cursing and ranting, but after a while calmed himself, pouring a stiff whiskey, and taking a German automatic pistol from a drawer. He checked its loads and tucked it into the inside pocket of his jacket. He went downstairs and

137

saw his new bodyguards, Harry Polanski and Spike Rogers, sprawled at a corner table.

'You boys are coming with me,' he said. 'Make sure your carbines are primed.'

Twelve

Shelby's Hotel was a run-down joint on a corner amid warehouses, along from the loading corrals for the railroad. It being rodeo it was practically deserted.

The clerk, a pasty-faced little man in a celluloid collar and shirtsleeves, put the telephone back on its hook, and simpered, 'She's waiting fer you. First floor, fourth room on right, number three. I put a bottle of Frenchie champagne on ice like you said.'

'Thanks.' Buck took the bottle in its bucket. 'How much I owe you?'

'Fifteen bucks. Rooms are scarce. It's rodeo week.'

Buck flipped him a golden eagle. 'Keep the change.'

The clerk gave a snigger. 'Hope the lady's worth it.'

'So do I,' Buck muttered, as he climbed the stairs and went along the gloomy corridor. 'Fourth on right, number three.' The door was unlocked and he stepped inside. 'Howdy, Rowena.'

'Hi, cowboy.' She was lying on one elbow on the none-too-clean coverlet, wearing a purple and gold striped basque, from the cups of which her extremely large and flaccid breasts spilled. 'I ain't chancin' gittin' in the sheets. Why choose this flea-bitten hole?'

'Waal,' he grinned as he popped the champagne and poured two glasses. 'I could hardly meetcha at The Plainsman.'

'You coulda come up. My old man will be out judgin' the ladies' equitation.'

'Aincha worried about missing Rachel?'

'I can see that spoiled bitch any day.' She clinked glasses with him and smiled her wide painted lips. 'This is a rare opportunity I didn't want to miss.'

Buck flipped his hat away, peeled off his two-tone shirt and eased himself on to the bed beside her. 'Waal, at last we git to meet in the flesh, Rowena. I been looking forward to this.'

The French corselette bulged out tight over the middle-aged woman's belly. She really wore it to cover the stretch marks and wrinkles. She wore no pantalettes. Black silk stockings were gartered above her knees revealing rather flabby thighs. She finished the drink too eagerly and sneezed. 'The bubbles got up my nose.'

'That ain't the only thang gonna git up your nose,' Buck drawled with a smile.

Rowena leaned over him to replace her glass on the bedside table. 'Promises. C'mon, cowboy.' She began to unbuckle his belt. 'Let's git on with it. Get your boots off.'

'Have another one, sweetheart. There ain't no hurry. We got all afternoon.' He refilled her glass and passed it to her. 'I'm a man who likes to keep his boots on.'

'Yeah?' She gave him a puzzled look but accepted

the champagne and guzzled at it. 'That's OK by me as long as you deliver the goods.'

Buck put his left arm around her shoulders and bobbed one of her breasts in his hand, like a man weighing a melon in a market place. 'I'm a man who likes to relax before he gets started.'

'Yeah? Well don't relax for too long. I ain't come to this dump to have you pass out on me.'

'Gawd,' he sighed, 'you're really something, Rowena. Doncha have any worries about cheatin' on your husband?'

'Not with you, I don't. You should see that fat flabby louse in the nude. He's got hairs all over his back. Now, you' – she put the glass aside again and ran her fingers over his smooth, bronzed torso and down his muscle-rippling abdomen – 'you're like you been carved from bronze.'

'Heck.' He laughed and wriggled back as her fingers clawed down into his jeans. 'Hey, I'm spilling my drink.'

'That ain't all I'm gonna make you spill. Come on,' she pleaded, as he swung off the bed, 'let's get on with it. What's the matter with you?'

'I like to git to know a lady first,' Buck said, tipping up the bottle by its neck and taking a pull. 'I'm funny like that.'

'Well, for Chris'sakes get to know me. I'm beginning to figure you famous rodeo riders ain't all you're cracked up to be. What's the matter, a bull get your balls?'

'I like a lady to be ladylike, Rowena. I kinda hoped you might be.'

'Come on, Buck, don't tease me like this. We both

know what we're here for.'

'Yeah,' he grinned, leaning over to kiss her capacious lips, 'I'm gonna take my boots off as a special treat for you. You know, I don't think your husband likes me.'

'You can say that again.' He had passed her the bottle and her words were getting slurred as she took another slug. 'To tell you the truth, I think he's been trying to kill you.'

'So, it was him.'

'Well, who you think pays Snake Stevens?'

'You don't say? He really must want Dusty to win.'

'Yeah, and Rachel.'

'Well, he ain't had much luck so far, has he, Mrs Rudge?'

'Hey, take your jeans off, let me have a look at you.'

Buck stretched his arms, smiled at her, and began to unpop his studs. He padded barefoot to the window and glanced out.

'Hell,' he drawled. 'Looks like we got company arriving.'

'Who?' she squawked.

'Your husband. An' a coupla gunslingers.' He took his Smith & Wesson and shoved it under a pillow. 'Maybe I'll be needing this.'

'Oh, my God,' she whispered. 'Does he look angry?'

'You can say that again.'

She sat up in bed, covering her trembling breasts with her hands, as if this might make them less conspicuous. 'What are we gonna do?' she said, in a croaking voice.

142

'It's a damn bad hand.' Buck bounced back on to the mattress beside her and hugged her into him. 'There ain' no use goin' out the window. What a nuisance, I got the bull-riding tomorrow.'

'Is that all you think of?'

'Just when you'd got me aroused, too. Must be them pale thighs of yourn.' He could hear footsteps clomping up the stairs and along the corridor. 'You don't know what they do to a man.'

He suddenly spotted a beady eye watching them through a small hole bored in the plasterboard wall. 'Oh, no,' he groaned. 'Looks like we got a peeper next door, too.'

Jane Merriman saddled Snow Storm as if in a trance, put on his double bridle, the bridoon, snaffle and bit, which would make him flex his neck, relax his lower jaw and collect himself. She adjusted the silly golden helmet on her head, with its ribbons which would trail out behind her in the breeze.

'Here goes,' she said to Reno. 'Give me a leg up.'

'You OK?'

'I guess.' She met his dark concerned eyes and tried to stifle the tears that wanted to well up in her own. 'I shoulda known better than to fall for a lousy rodeo rider, shouldn't I?'

She swung into the saddle and arranged her gauzy dress. Rachel Rudge had gone first and completed a competent round, although she kept glancing into the audience as if searching for her absent parents. Perhaps that had made her drop some points. Or, perhaps, she just wasn't a mature enough rider.

There was a smattering of applause for a middle-aged woman rider called Jane Gaunt. Gaunt by name and gaunt by nature, bony and severe in an English-style black riding outfit, a bowler hat pulled hard down over her unsmiling features. She was not popular with the crowd, but had performed a near-perfect round. She would be Jane's main rival.

But what did she care any more? She wished she had never come to Oklahoma City. It was as if all her feelings had been blunted. She wished she had never met the double-crossing Buck Bradley. Well, she had only herself to blame. But, for moments, for days, she had believed in him. And now he had brought it all crashing down around her. Why? her mind kept repeating. Why? For God's sake, why?

Jane went through the series of tests like an automaton. She had practised so hard, so long, they came as second nature to her. The audience was just a blur as she rode around the arena. She did not give a damn about them. Snow Storm really needed little guidance. He, too, was hoof-perfect. First they went through the collected paces: trot, canter, walk, forwards, reverse, sideways, and off again at a kind of walking trot. The Appaloosa was so proud and haughty. Because his mistress's emotions were numbed she did not communicate any nervousness to him. He, however, made one serious mistake performing the sideways movement: he skipped and shied, too fast, too far. The point of the exercise was so that a horse would avoid a snake basking on the ground. He seemed as if he had really spotted one.

Jane was forced to concentrate and he recovered his equilibrium. 'Come on, boy.' She leaned forward to pat his neck. 'You can do this.' She put him into the final racking number, a difficult, single-footed pace when each foot has to come down alone and at speed in turn. He pranced along the arena to rapturous applause. She hardly noticed it.

'How did I do?' she asked Reno, as she jumped down.

'Good. You're only two points behind the Gaunt lady.'

Jane released Snow Storm's restricting head harness and kissed his nose. 'You're the only creature in the world I can rely on,' she said. 'Well' - she turned to Reno - 'it looks like she's won.'

'It ain't over yet. There's tomorrow's jumpin' to come. Then Buck'll be in the bull-ridin'.'

'Oh, yes, the bull-riding. I hope he breaks his damn neck.'

Buck pulled Rowena across the front of him as Harry Polanski kicked in the bedroom door and Robert Rudge came through with a new-fangled automatic pistol in his grip, pointed at them. Not a very gentlemanly thing of Buck to do, but at least it stopped Rudge shooting for a few seconds. Rowena screamed. 'Don't!'

'Why not, you adulterous whore? I've a mind to kill you both. How could you do this to me, Rowena?'

Polanski had a Wimchester carbine in his hands, grinning as he covered them. 'Caught 'em, ain't we?'

Rudge's dark-bearded face was grim and his hand was shaking. It was a tense situation. 'Put my wife to one side, Bradley. You're gonna get what you deserve.'

Buck still had his left arm around Rowena's bare shoulders as he tried a bluff. 'You ain't got the nerve to kill me, Rudge. You get others to do your killing for you, like Snake Stevens. He mighta shot that railroad conductor and the poor damn preacher by mistake, but you sure as hell paid him to.'

'Don't be so sure, mister.' Rudge took first pressure on the trigger. 'Nobody would hang me for killin' you. This is gonna be what they call a crime of passion.'

'Aw, what you gettin' so het up about, Rudge? She came here of her own free will. Anyhow, there's another thang you don't know,' he lied, 'they fished that crazy hill-billy out from under the falls and he says it was Snake who talked him into killing them three cowboys and kidnapping the girl. So, that's down to you. You'll hang, all right. Unless, of course, I keep my mouth shut.'

'You'll keep your mouth shut, Bradley. You won't be saying another word.' Rudge faltered for moments. It was true, he was not a man who liked to do his own killing close-up. 'You're forgetting who holds all the cards. Sure, I put Snake up to it. He fouled up, but my friend Harry here ain't going to. Get dressed, cowboy. We're taking you for a ride out on the prairie and you ain't coming back. Come oh, move it.'

'You don't have to kill him, Bob,' his wife protested. 'Don't be a fool.'

'He's asked for it.'

'Why don't you just break his legs like you did that other man who owed you money?'

'Shut up, Rowena. You get dressed, too. No, he's

got to die. He knows too much. I don't trust this sonuvagun. Keep him covered, Harry. He's a slippery customer. We'll take him out to the Big Rock. By the time they find him the buzzards'll have had their fill.'

'Come on, Bradley,' Harry growled. 'Let's go.'

Suddenly the thin, plank partition wall of the bedroom was smashed apart and a big man crashed through gripping a carbine in his hands. Harry Polanski swung his own Winchester to fire at him, but the big man smashed a slug into his chest. Polanski tumbled back, his shirt flowering blood.

The startled oilman, Rudge, snapped off a shot from his automatic, the bullet whistling past Buck's ear. The cowboy whipped his revolver from beneath the pillow and fired fast. The bullet creased Rudge's knuckles and he dropped the automatic like it was red hot.

Rudge stared at them for a second, then turned to run out to the landing and down the corridor. Buck followed, firing a shot, but Rudge had started down the stairs. Bradley reached the top and put his third .44 through his thigh. Rudge went tumbling and crashing to lie groaning beside the startled clerk.

'You took your time, didn't you, Marshal?'

'I had to hear what he said,' Sam Gray grunted, as he joined him. 'A clear admission of guilt.'

Rudge had managed to get to his feet and was hopping out of the hotel doorway, holding his thigh. Buck sent another shot crashing after him and dived down the stairs two at a time. He knelt in the doorway and looked outside. 'Halt,' he shouted.

Rudge was trying to climb into the buggy. 'Get him!' he screamed.

His other bodyguard, Spike Rogers, appeared on the flat roof of the warehouse opposite. Buck had forgotten about him. He rolled for cover behind a water trough, returning fire as Rogers' carbine blazed and bullets splintered the sidewalk

'Come on out, Bradley,' Spike shouted. 'Why don't you stand up and face me? Or are you all out of lead?'

Buck wasn't sure. Had he spent five? Or six? He swallowed his fear and stood to face Spike, the Smith & Wesson dangling in his fist. 'Why don't you try me?'

Spike grinned as if this was going to be easy, raised the carbine and it spat flame. He stood looking down at the rodeo star who had raised his revolver. His smile turned to a snarl of anger and agony. 'You win,' he hissed, and pivoted forward, crashing on his back on the street, his blood staining his shirt around the heart. Buck's sixth bullet had been spot on.

Robert Rudge had watched the duel with fascinated horror as the seconds passed. But he had the reins in his hands and whipped the pair of milk-white horses forward. 'Haagh!'

Deputy US Marshal Sam Gray poked his carbine through the hotel bedroom window. One shot sent Rudge rolling into the dust as the terrified horses raced away.

Bradley, barechested, stood barefoot in the dust. 'Whoo'.' He grinned. 'I weren't sure if I had a last slug left.'

Rowena emerged from the hotel, back in her flouncy dress and straw hat, followed by the grey-suited Sam Gray.

'Looks like they all gone to the happy huntin''

148

ground,' Buck drawled, poking the lifeless Rudge with his toe. 'Jeez, one slug can sure make a mess of a man, cain't it? Look at all that blood.'

'The hangman's been robbed of his fee,' Gray said. 'But it saves me some paperwork.' He turned to Rowena and pointed a finger at her. 'I ain't charging you with complicity in these events, Mrs Rudge, but let this be a warning. I'll go try to catch your buggy for you.'

Rowena stared down at her husband's corpse, turned and tried to claw the rodeo rider's face, screaming insults and obscenities. Buck caught her arm. 'He kinda brought this on himself, Rowena. Why you so worried? You'll be a rich widder. Or maybe you're disappointed we didn't do nuthin'?'

'You lousy bastard,' she hissed and spat in his face. 'You set me up.'

'Waal' – he wiped the spittle away and pushed her aside - 'we had to do somethang. I better go git dressed. Uh, by the way, I think you're wrong there. I'm purty sure my mammy and daddy was married when I come along.'

Thirteen

Jane Merriman rode like a dream in the ladies final. In her flowing show dress and helmet she floated over the fences. Snow Storm gave a spirited, precision-perfect performance, responding to his mistress' sensitive hands. But he was still behind on points from his mistake in the equitation events. Mrs Gaunt, riding next, made a masterly round and retained her lead. Rachel Rudge, in spite of her fine horse, came in a poor fifth. Perhaps it was the upset over her father's death, or simply inexperience.

Rachel did better in the deciding event, the obstacle course, more of a wild hurly-burly into which she threw her horse foolhardily. Jane, instead, lost seconds by holding Snow Storm back. His natural urge as the crowd roared was to go like a cannonball. Jane carefully collected him but he surged through the assorted barrels, fences and posts, nonetheless. It looked like they would take second place. However, unfortunately for Jane Gaunt, she came a cropper, cornering too fast and demolishing one of the doubles, her mount slithering to his knees, and Mrs Gaunt thrown over his head to land in a humiliating tangle on her back-side.

Jane could hardly believe it. She had won. She took a turn of honour around the arena with a smile of appreciation of the crowd's cheers. She rode up to the rostrum to receive the golden challenge bowl and the thousand dollars prize as Horse Woman of the year. Mrs Rowena Rudge, dressed in black, gave her an icy glare.

When she rode out of the arena she saw Buck joining in the applause. She took off her helmet and tossed her hair back, haughtily, ignoring him. She booked a room in the Plainsman Hotel and when he came banging on her door she telephoned down to the manager and requested that a drunken pest of a rodeo rider be tossed out into the street.

'Why you doin' this, Janey?' he yelled.

'You did it to me,' she whispered, more to herself. 'You got me all wrong.'

'Go away. I've got a date for dinner with a rich old rancher. What's good for the goose, as they say. Who needs you, cowboy?'

Sporting a black eye, and a massive hangover, Buck was not his customary cheerful self for the final day's events. Dusty pipped him again at the pony races. And in the bronco-riding he drew a wall-eyed mustang, as nasty-natured as he looked.

'Git ready to have your hat flattened,' Reno grinned.

Buck rosinned his glove and grunted. 'We'll see.' He gave his familiar high-pitched yell as the wall-eye shotgunned out of the stall. There was hardly time

151

to think, no time for fear as the bronco went into his high-kicking, bucking routine across the arena. Buck gripped with his right hand and fanned the air with his left for balance, lashed back and forth with such virulence it was as if his head was going to be torn from his shoulders. Uh-huh, he groaned mentally, as he realized the mustang was aimed full-on for the high barricade, intent to crash his side against it, wipe this man from his back. He had split-seconds to hook his boot over the bronco's plunging neck and leap for safety. He did a flying run, landed on his feet . . . and watched the wall-eye go bucking on his way.

'It ain't fair,' he muttered, as he picked up his hat. 'That hoss had a grudge against me.'

Dusty Roberts didn't do a lot better, pile-driving his head into the baked mud. Now the two rivals were equal.

Bronco-busting might be fast and furious, but it was relatively safe. In bull-riding a man could easily get himself killed. Buck could not ignore a sense of dread as the evening approached. The tar flares were lit around the arena, and the crowd seemed to sense the riders' apprehension. The bull-riding was the grand finale of the Oklahoma City rodeo. Buck groaned at his aching bones and said to Reno, 'I'm beginning to think it's time I quit this game.'

'If a man thinks of his fear,' Reno replied, 'then it is time.'

'I ain't sceered,' Buck protested, 'it's just like this is crazy.' As if fore-ordained he had drawn his old adversary, Angelface. By comparison the other contestants would have it easy. 'Why me?' he groaned.

Angelface was in the chute and had started kicking and snorting his fury. What bull wouldn't be angry with a rope tied taut around its testicles? Maybe it *was* a cruel sport. But the beast only suffered for a matter of minutes then it was back to the pasture and mating with the cows until his next challenge came along. His rider might be crippled for life.

Buck had to ride the most feared and demonic old warrior on the circuit. He tried to put the image of Curly being kicked to death, of Lance's dull eyes, of Merriman's wheelchair, out of his mind, but his heart pounded as he climbed on to the chute. He looked around the arena and saw Jane sitting, cool and beautiful in a summer dress, in a box beside the rich rancher. So, she was still freezing him out?

'She mighta wished me luck,' he muttered, as he performed the ritual wind of the rope around his palm and lowered himself on to nearly a ton of hot, raging beast. But the thought of her made him reckless and he yelled, 'Let's go!' He jerked down his hatbrim, nodded to the men on the gate, and Angelface blasted out of the chute like a bomb, scattering arena dust in a cloud as he went into an instant heart-stopping belly-roll and spun, simultaneously, into a great jack-knife of a sky-high jump. Buck felt air between him and the brahma's back as he was catapulted forward over his powerful hump. He battled to combat the bull's strength and rage and regained his balance. Angelface's hooves hit terra firma and powered him angrily into another twisting, kicking spin, shaking his body like some hootchy-kootchy dancer.

All Buck could hear was the earsplitting roar of the crowd in his ears. All he could do was clench his muscles and hang on. Until - oh no, there was an ominous gasp from the crowd - his balance went and he was somersaulted forwards to land under the bull's horns and hooves.

A viciously spiked horn caught him in the groin, picking him up like a rag doll and tossing him to one side. The bull's eyes and mouth were like a fiery, belching volcano as he returned to the attack . . . but the brave clowns rushed in, waving coloured capes to distract him. Angelface turned to chase them, as Buck was dragged towards the safety of the rails.

At least, it seemed like safety until he looked up and saw a man jump into the arena and plough across the dust towards him. The big hat, beard and duster coat could not disguise the cadaverous face and snakelike eyes of Snake Stevens and he was pulling out a Remington revolver. . . .

'I'm gonna finish the damn bull's job,' he shouted. 'I waited a long time for this.'

Buck, unarmed, pleaded for a gun from one of the men who had jumped in to drag him from the arena, and rolled to one side, the pain in his groin tearing through him. Stevens' first shot spat into the dust beside him. Suddenly Snake spun around, an arrow piercing his shoulder. He saw Reno perched on the chute rail, fixing another arrow into his bow. Snake fanned out two bullets and toppled the part-Comanche. 'Take that, you lousy redskin.'

He returned to the attack on the fallen rodeo rider. But someone had pressed a Colt. 45 into Buck's hand. He thumbed the hammer and they fired, simultaneously. Snake's bullet hit Buck like the kick from a mule and he felt his senses swimming. Before blackness closed in on him he saw Snake clutch at his chest and topple into the dust. 'I just had to finish the job,' Stevens said, as he coughed blood: 'Hot damn! What happened to my lucky dollar?'

'Where am I?' Buck asked, sometime later, as he regained consciousness. He was lying on a stretcher, looking up at a constellation of stars. A slim face silhouetted beneath a straw sombrero was coming closer and a pair of serious, violet-blue eyes were illumined by the flares. 'What happened?' He groaned at the pain in his shoulder and upper thigh. 'Am I dead and gone to heaven?'

'No, you killed him. Snake's dead.'

'How about Reno?'

'He's gonna be OK. The doc says neither of you has lost any of your vital organs. Thank goodness.'

'Angelface?'

'You rode him to a count of ten, honey.' A pair of tender, moist and promising lips touched his. 'Reno told me why you went to see the Rudge woman. I'm sorry I doubted you.'

'So, who won?'

'You did, cowboy. You're Oklahoma champion.'

'You mean I did it?'

'You sure did, cowboy. You think we can go home now?'

'What happened to your boyfriend?'

155

'Aw, his wife turned up in town.'

Buck grinned at her and opened his arms. 'Just git me up off this thang. I gotta go collect my prize. Then we're headin' for the Lazy River ranch, Jane. And we won't be comin' back.'